THE INDUSTRIAL REPUBLIC

A volume in the Hyperion reprint series
THE RADICAL TRADITION IN AMERICA

HYPERION PRESS, INC.
Westport, Connecticut

Courtesy of Everybody's Magazine

"VOORUIT"
Home of the Socialist Societies of Ghent

The Industrial Republic

A Study of the America of
Ten Years Hence

By
UPTON SINCLAIR

ILLUSTRATED

New York
Doubleday, Page & Company
1907

Published in 1907 by Doubleday, Page & Company, New York
Copyright 1907 by Doubleday, Page & Company
Hyperion reprint edition 1976
Reproduced from a copy in the collection of Southern Illinois
University Libraries, Carbondale, Illinois
Library of Congress Catalog Number 75-344
ISBN 0-88355-248-5
Printed in the United States of America

Library of Congress Cataloging in Publication Data

Sinclair, Upton Beall, 1878-1968.
   The industrial republic : a study of the America of
ten years hence.

   (The Radical tradition in America)
   Reprint of the ed. published by Doubleday, Page,
New York.
   1. Socialism in the United States. 2. United
States — Economic conditions — 1865-1918. 3. United
States — Social conditions — 1865-1918. I. Title.
HX86.S62   1976   335'.00973   75-344
ISBN 0-88355-248-5

TO H. G. WELLS
"THE NEXT MOST HOPEFUL"

INTRODUCTION

The thought of the time has familiarised us with the evolutionary view of things; we understand that life is the product of an inner impulse, labouring to embody itself in the world of sense; and that the product is always changing—that there is nothing permanent save the principles and laws in accordance with which development goes on. We understand that the universe of things was evolved by slow stages into what it is to-day, that all life has come into being in the same way. We have traced this process in the far-distant suns and in the strata of the earth; we have traced it in the vegetables and in the animals, in the seed and in the embryo; we have traced it in all of man's activities, his ways of thinking and acting, of eating and dressing and working and fighting and praying.

This book is an attempt to interpret in the light of evolutionary science the social problem of our present world; to consider American institutions as they exist at this hour—what forces are now at work within them, and what changes they are likely to produce. The subject-matter dealt with is not abstract speculation, but rather the everyday realities of the world we know—our present political parties and public men, our present corporations and captains of industry, our present labour unions and newspapers, colleges and churches. The thing sought is an answer to a concrete and definite question: *What will America be ten years from now?*

Inasmuch as the people who are most interested in practical affairs are very busy people, I judge it to be a common-sense procedure to set forth my ideas in miniature at the outset; so that one may learn in two or three minutes exactly what my book contains, and judge whether he cares to read it.

It is my belief that the student of a generation from now will look back upon the last two centuries of human history and interpret them as the final stage of a long process whereby man was transformed from a solitary and predatory individual to a social and peaceable member of a single world community. He will see that men, pressed by the struggle for existence, had united themselves into groups under the discipline of laws and conventions; and that the last two centuries represented the period when these laws and conventions, having done their unifying work, and secured the survival of the group, were set aside and replaced by free and voluntary social effort.

Introduction

The student will furthermore perceive that this evolutionary process had two manifestations, two waves, so to speak; the first political, and the second industrial; the first determined by man's struggle to protect his life, and the second by his struggle to amass wealth. The culmination of the first occurred successively in the English revolutions, the American and French revolutions, and the other various efforts after political freedom. After each of these achievements the historian notices a period of bitterness and disillusionment, a sense of failure, it being discovered that the expected did not occur, that Liberty, Equality and Fraternity did not become the rule of men's conduct. After that, however, succeeds a period of enlightenment, it having been realised that the work has only been half done, that man has been made only half free. The political sovereignty has been taken out of the possession of private individuals and made the property of the whole community, to be shared in by all upon equal terms; but the industrial sovereignty still remains the property of a few. A man can no longer be put in jail or taxed by a king, but he can be starved and exploited by a master; his body is now his own, but his labour is another's—and there is very little difference between the two. So immediately there begins a new movement, the end of which is a new revolution, and the establishment of THE INDUSTRIAL REPUBLIC.

What do I mean by an Industrial Republic? I mean an organisation for the production and distribution of wealth, whose members are established upon a basis of equality; who elect representatives to govern the organisation; and who receive the full value of what their labour produces. I mean an industrial government of the people, by the people, for the people; a community in which the means of production have been made the inalienable property of the State. My purpose in writing this book is to point out the forces which are now rapidly developing in America; and which, when they have attained to maturity, will usher in the Industrial Republic by a process as natural and as inevitable as that by which a chick breaks out of its shell or a child comes forth from the womb at the proper hour. I believe that the economic process is whirling us on with terrific momentum toward the crisis; and I look to see the most essential features of the great transformation accomplished in America within one year after the Presidential election of 1912.

If I had been a tactful person I should have kept that last statement until far on in my argument. For I find many people who are interested in the idea of an Industrial Republic, and some few who are willing

Introduction

to think of it as a possibility; but I find none who do not balk when I presume to set the day. Yet the setting of the day is a vital part of my conviction, and I should play the reader false if I failed to mention it in this preliminary statement of my argument. It is a conviction to which I have come with the diligent use of the best faculties I possess, and after a preparation of a sort that is certainly unusual, and possibly even quite unique.

Perhaps I cannot do better by way of introduction than to explain just what I mean. Our country has passed through two great crises, when important political and social changes came with startling suddenness. I refer to the Revolution and the Civil War; and to the latter of these crises, or rather the period of its preparation —1847 to 1861—I once had occasion to give two years of an interesting kind of study. I read everything which I could find in the two largest special collections in the country; not merely histories and biographies, but the documents of the time, speeches and sermons and letters, newspapers and magazines and pamphlets. I literally lived in the period; I knew it more intimately than the world that was actually about me. My purpose was to write a novel which should make the crisis real to the people of the present; and so I had to read creatively, I had to get into the very soul of what I read. I had to struggle and to suffer with the people of that time, to forget my knowledge of the future, and to watch through their eyes the hourly unfolding of the mighty drama of events.

There were so many kinds of men—statesmen and business men, lawyers and clergymen, heroes and cowards; and I had to study them all, and see the thing through the eyes of each of them. And of course, I could only play at ignorance, for I knew the future; and I saw all their mistakes, and the reasons for them, and the pity and the folly and the tragedy of it all. Knowing, as I did, the great underlying forces which were driving behind the events, I saw all these people as puppets, moved here and there by powers of whose existence they never dreamed.

And, of course, all the while I was also reading my morning newspaper, and watching the world of to-day; and inevitably I found myself testing the people of the present by these same methods. I would find myself seeking for the forces which were at work to-day, and striving to reach out to the future to which they were leading. I would find myself, by the way of helping in this interpretation, comparing and balancing the two eras, and transposing its leading figures back and forth. This famous educator or this newspaper editor of to-day—what would he have been saying had he lived in 1852? And this clergyman friend of mine, this politician—where would he fit into that period? Or if Yancey had been alive to-day, what would he have been doing? Where should I have found Seward—what parts would Edward Everett and Wendell Phillips and Jefferson Davis have been playing?

It was really a fascinating problem in proportion. The men of fifty years ago stood thus and so to a known crisis; similar men of the present stand thus to an unknown crisis—and now find the crisis. When I had finished "Manassas" I took up the writing of "The Jungle"; which is simply to say that I was drawn on irresistibly to seek for this latter crisis, and to try to understand it—to get into the heart of it, and live it and follow it to its end, just as I had done with the earlier one. So now I feel that I have much the same sort of power as Cuvier, the naturalist, who could construct a prehistoric animal from a bit of its bone. I have far more than the bone of this monster—I have his tail, beginning far back in the seventies; and I have the whole of his huge body—the present. I have counted his scales and measured his limbs; I have even felt his pulse and had his blood under the microscope. And now you ask me—How many more vertebræ will there be in the neck of this strange animal? And what will be the size and the shape of his head?

So it is that I write in all seriousness that the revolution will take place in America within one year after the Presidential election of 1912; and, in saying this, I claim to speak, not as a dreamer nor as a child, but as a scientist and a prophet.

CONTENTS

		PAGE
Introduction		vii

CHAPTER		
I.	The Coming Crisis	3
II.	Industrial Evolution	27
III.	Markets and Misery	72
IV.	Social Decay	103
V.	Business and Politics	138
VI.	The Revolution	179
VII.	The Industrial Republic	215

ILLUSTRATIONS

"Vooruit," Home of the Socialist societies of
Ghent . . . . . *Frontispiece*

                                     FACING PAGE

A Socialist view of the Trusts . . . 48

Reaping by hand and by machinery . . 92

Child labor in glass factories and coal mines 114

The Social contrast in New York . . . 126

Coxey's Army on the march and in Washington 206

The competitive vs. coöperative distribution
of information 220

Helicon Hall 274

THE INDUSTRIAL REPUBLIC

THE INDUSTRIAL REPUBLIC

CHAPTER I

THE COMING CRISIS

THE thing which most impresses the student of the Civil War struggle, is how generally and completely the people who lived through it failed to understand it themselves. We of the present day know that the War was a clash between two incompatible types of civilisation; between an agricultural and conservative aristocracy, and a commercial and progressive democracy. We can see that each society developed in its people a separate point of view, separate customs and laws, ideals and policies, literatures and religions. We can see that their differing interests as to tariffs, police regulations, domestic improvements and foreign affairs, made political strife between them inevitable; and that finally the expansion which was necessary to the life of each brought them into a conflict which could only end with the submission of one or the other. Yet, plain as this seems to us now, the people of that time did not grasp it; through the whole long process they were dragged, as it were, by the hair of their heads, and each event as it came was a separate phenomenon, a fresh source of astonishment, alarm, and indignation. Even after the war had broken out, the vast majority of them would not be enlightened as in regard to it—a few of them have not been enlightened yet. I talked recently with an old Confederate naval officer, who said to me: "Oh, yes; it was the politicians who made the war." I recall the astonished look which crossed the old gentleman's face when I ventured the opinion that the politicians of this country had never yet made anything except their own livings.

It seemed not merely that they *could* not understand the thing; they *would* not. The truth did not please them, and the best and wisest of them appeared to have the idea that they had only not to see it, and it would cease to be the truth; after the manner of the learned men of Galileo's time, who declined to look through his telescope, or to watch him drop weights from the Tower of Pisa. They made it a matter of offence that anyone should understand; the ability to predict political events was held to imply some collusion with them. When Lincoln, just before the crash, ventured to doubt the stability of "a house divided against itself," his enemies fell upon him precisely

The Coming Crisis

as if he had declared, not that such a house would fall, but that he intended to knock it down. And this was the established view of all the conservatism of the country, only two or three years before there burst upon it one of the most fearful cataclysms of history.

Let us endeavour to place ourselves in the position of the average man of 1860, and see how the whole matter appeared to him.

Way back in the early thirties, eight or ten more or less insane fanatics—"apostate priests and unsexed women," as one writer described them—had got together and begun an agitation for a wholly impossible and visionary (to say nothing of revolutionary and unconstitutional) programme—"the immediate and unconditional emancipation of the slaves." They formed a society and started a paper called the *Liberator*. When governors of Southern states protested concerning it, the Hon. Harrison Gray Otis, Mayor of Boston, wrote as follows: "It appeared upon inquiry that no member of the city government, nor any person of my acquaintance, had ever heard of the publication. Sometime afterward it was reported to me by the city officers that they had ferreted out the paper and its editor; that his office was an obscure hole, his only visible auxiliary a negro boy, and his supporters a very few ignorant persons of all colours. This information, with the consent of the Aldermen, I communicated to the above named governors, with an utterance of my belief that the new fanaticism had not made, nor was likely to make, proselytes among the respectable classes of the people."

Nevertheless, the danger of this propaganda was recognised, and before long the Abolitionists were being stoned and shot, their presses smashed, and their meetings broken up; a "broadcloth mob" put a rope round the neck of the editor of the *Liberator* and dragged him through the streets of the city. And still, in spite of this, the agitation went on. All the "cranks" of the country gradually rallied about the movement. Their leader was a woman's suffragist, an infidel, a prohibitionist, and a vegetarian; he denounced the Constitution as "an agreement with Death, and a covenant with Hell." There was one man among them who addressed meetings with clanking chains about his wrists, and a three-pronged iron slave-collar about his neck; and who declared to the people of a town that they "had better establish among them a hundred rum-shops, fifty gambling-houses and ten brothels, than one church." They allowed Negroes to speak on the platform with them, and they opened schools for Negro girls, or tried to, until these were

The Coming Crisis

broken up. One of them refused to pay taxes to a slave-holding government, and went to jail for it.

Assuredly, no common-sense person would have thought that here was anything save a madness that might be allowed to run its course. Yet the Abolitionists kept at it. In the election of 1840, a wing of them split off, and nominated a candidate for the Presidency, who received seven thousand votes out of a total of two or three millions. Four years later, when the Democratic Party was on the verge of forcing the country into a war with Mexico, they raised a hue and cry that this was a "slave-driver's enterprise," with the result that their vote went up to sixty-two thousand. And by keeping up the ceaseless agitation all through the war, and taking advantage of a factional quarrel in New York state to nominate a politician who came into their camp for the sake of revenge, they cast, in 1848, a vote of two hundred and ninety-one thousand.

And also they had by this time succeeded in colouring a great mass of the popular thought with their views. They had gotten the country unsettled; they had made people feel that something was wrong, and all sorts of anti-slavery measures were beginning to be championed. Some wanted to exclude slavery from the new Territories; some wanted to exclude it from the National

Capital; some wanted to restrict the domestic slave-trade. All of these people, of course, denied indignantly that they were Abolitionists, denied that they had any sympathy with Abolitionism, or that their measures had anything to do with it. But the South, whom the matter concerned, understood perfectly well the folly of such a claim—understood that the institution of Slavery was one which could not be made war upon, or limited, and that the first hostile move which was made against it would necessarily mean its downfall. Hence, to the South, all these people were "Abolitionists."

Over the California question, there came at last a crisis, and all the Conservative forces of the nation were scarcely equal to the settling of it. Edward Everett and Rufus Choate and Calhoun and Clay and Webster, and a dozen others that one might name, exerted all their influence, and went about warning their countrymen of the danger, and denouncing what Webster called "the din and roll and rub-a-dub of Abolition presses and Abolition lectures." Under these circumstances the "Compromise" was adopted, and the vote of the Abolitionist Party fell off to one hundred and fifty-six thousand.

But then came the repeal of the Missouri Compromise, which brought Lincoln into politics. The Abolition clamour surged up

The Coming Crisis   9

as never before—here was one proof the more, they said, that Slavery was menacing American institutions. The whole country seemed suddenly to be full of their supporters; and the Kansas Raid only added more fuel to the flame. The Republican Party was formed, the *Black* Republican Party, as the slave-holders called it; and at the Presidential election of 1856, they cast more than one million three hundred thousand votes, about one-third of the total vote of the country.

After that came, in due course, the attempt of the Supreme Court to put an end to the Abolitionist agitation, declaring that Congress could not restrict slavery in the Territories, which meant that the Republican Party had no right to exist. To "cheerfully acquiesce" in the decision of the Supreme Court, was the duty of "all good citizens," according to President Buchanan; yet the only result of the action of the Supreme Court was to cause the agitation to burst out afresh. In Illinois, Abraham Lincoln ran for senator in flat defiance of the Supreme Court's decision, and the Republican Party all over the country went on in its revolutionary course, precisely as if no Supreme Court had ever existed. A year or two later an agitator made matters still worse by his attempt to set free the slaves by force. "It is my firm and deliberate conviction," said

Senator Douglas, "that the Harper's Ferry crime was the natural, logical and inevitable result of the doctrines and teachings of the Republican Party." And he was perfectly right.

It was disgraceful, and yet it would not stop. The North had by this time become so full of Abolitionism, that even the Democrats were not to be trusted. When the split came, in Charleston, Yancey of Alabama explained this. "When I was a boy in the Northern States," he said, "Abolitionists were pelted with rotten eggs. But now this band of Abolitionists has spread and grown into three bands—the Black Republicans, the Free-soilers, and the Squatter-sovereignty men—all representing the common sentiment that Slavery is wrong." And when Abraham Lincoln was elected President by a minority of the people, upon a platform which declared that the Constitution was to be disregarded, the party of conservatism and tradition resorted to *force* to maintain its rights.

And what happened then? Why, simply this: a group of fanatical visionaries who had for thirty years been jeered at for demanding of the country something that was revolutionary and inconceivable—the destruction of an institution which had stood for centuries, and was built into the very framework of the nation—suddenly

The Coming Crisis

began to see the mighty structure totter, to see cracks open in it, to see its pillars crumble, its roof fall in; and at last, before they had fairly time to realise what was happening, the whole heaven-defying colossus lay a heap of dust and ruins at their feet!

I have said that I believe that our country is now only a few years away from a similar great transformation. In order to maintain that thesis, it will be necessary to show, first, a great underlying economic cause, working irresistibly to force the issue; and second, a consequent movement of protest, slowly making headway and ultimately permeating the whole thought of the country.

What was the cause of the Civil War? To put it into a phrase, it was the need under which Slavery laboured of securing new territory. The reader may find a contemporary exposition of the situation in Olmstead's "Cotton Kingdom." Slave labour was a very wasteful means of cultivation—only the top of the soil was used, and ten or fifteen crops exhausted it. Virginia was once a great exporting state, but in the forties and fifties it had become simply a slave-breeding ground for the younger generation, which had moved to the Far South. And then, when the Far South began to prove insufficient, there was

then come a time when the other pairs, having less and less, were finally unable to furnish as much profits as were necessary?

We began the economic battle in this country upon equal terms. Some got the advantage and became masters, the others becoming wage-workers. This advantage —that is, capital—brought constantly increasing advantage—profit, rent, interest; and those who had not the advantage stayed meanwhile just where they were— they got enough to live on, and no more. Numerous exceptions to this do not in the least disturb the main facts—that as a class the wage-workers stayed wage-workers, and the masters stayed masters. Neither does the fact that wages rose constantly in the least disturb the main fact, for the cost of living rose also; the wage-worker got his living then, and he gets it now. And meanwhile, according to the way of nature, and in spite of the outcry of moralists and old-fashioned statesmen, the strong went on growing stronger, and fighting among each other, the victors growing ten times stronger yet; until now we have come to a stage where, industrially speaking, we are a nation of eighty million pygmies and a dozen giants. Nor is the work quite done yet—it is going straight on, in spite of anti-trust decisions and the labour of the "muck-

stood, are fractions; and fractions may be decreased as well by increasing the denominator, as by decreasing the numerator. A man, for instance, who invested a hundred dollars and made six, would receive six per cent. interest; but if he invested the second year one hundred and six dollars, and was able still to gain only six, his profit would be, not six per cent., but only five and a fraction. If he wished to make six, he would have to squeeze out a little more than six dollars; would have to compel the man who paid it to him to work just a little harder. And that, in miniature, is a representation of what is going on in our society to-day. You, the well-meaning reader, who are struggling to make the world better, and failing—whether the thing which you are trying to reform be politics or literature or religion, New York or Colorado or the Philippines, Fifth Avenue or Wall Street or Hell's Kitchen—you are meeting with failure because of that little arithmetical difficulty which has just been set forth.

Consider our millionaire fortunes, how they grow. Consider, for instance, that Mr. John D. Rockefeller makes fifty per cent. a year upon his holdings in the Standard Oil Company. The stock of the Standard Oil Company is now at five hundred, and has been as high as eight hundred in the market. This is assuming that Mr.

Rockefeller invested in the stock at par—though as a matter of fact, he put in only about twenty dollars a share, which would make his profit two hundred and fifty per cent. His income is at least fifty million dollars a year.

What does he do with it? Of course, he can't spend it—if he treated himself to a St. Louis Exposition every year, he couldn't spend it. What he does with it is to take it promptly, and reinvest it in the form of new capital; he employs a staff of thirty-two trained experts to aid him in this work. The effect of this is, of course, to make his income fifty per cent., *compound* interest, instead of simple; and what it will be in the course of time is a problem for those who like figures. While he is doing this, all the other capitalists are doing the same—the American millionaire lets his wife and daughters spend as much of his money as they can, but he seldom spends any himself; he is more interested in "doing things." The consequence is, therefore, that year after year we are paying the vast mass of our people mere living wages, and all the surplus product of our toil we are selling, and devoting to the creation of new instruments of production. We have, mark you, machinery that creates products for hundreds of times as many men as it employs, and still we skim off the surplus and devote it to making new machines. Is it not obvious that this cannot go on forever? And that the time must come that we make all that we need—or rather that our people have money to buy, wages being what they are? And if that ever happens, then of course the factories will have to shut down. We shall have millions of men out of work, and starving on our streets; and when they form processions and begin agitating, demanding that we give them work, then we say—that is, our newspapers, our preachers, our politicians, everybody says—

"But, my good man, there is no more work to be done!"

"But I am starving," insists the workingman, "we are *all* starving. *Why* is there no work?"

"The reason there is no work is 'overproduction.' The market is clogged with products, you must understand, and we can't sell them. What is your trade?"

"I work in a shoe-factory."

"But the shoe market is already glutted—there are twice as many shoes as there is any use for."

"Twice as many shoes! But my feet are on the ground!"

"Well, we can't help that, my good man; that's because you have no money to buy them with."

"And my friend here," goes on the workingman—"he is a tailor, and he is naked because there are too many coats on the market?"

"Exactly."

"And the baker here is starving because we are both too poor to buy his bread?"

"Exactly."

"And then this druggist is sick because we have no money to buy medicine?"

"Exactly."

After which, the workingman stands and scratches his head for a moment. "There is too much of everything," he reflects. "There is no more work to be done." And suddenly the light breaks. "Oh, I see!" he cries, "we have finished our work for the capitalists!" And you answer, "Exactly! everything is complete, and of course there is no more room for you. Therefore you had best be off to another planet!"

So it would be, if the workingman were content to take his doctrines from the other side—from the retainers of those "to whom God in His Infinite Wisdom has entrusted the care of the property interests of the country." But, meantime, the workingman has been thinking for himself—and evolving a quite new doctrine, all his own, concerning the property interests of the country. This doctrine is, in a word, that the means of production of wealth belong of right to no individual, but to the whole people; and that in the hour of the collapse of the profit-making system, the thing for the people to do is to take possession of the machinery, and use it to produce goods, no longer for those who own, but for those who work.

And that brings me to the second of my tasks. I have shown the "great underlying economic cause, working irresistibly to force the issue"; there remains to show the consequent "movement of protest."

I have before me, as I write, a little pamphlet published by the Standard Publishing Company," of Terre Haute, Indiana, and entitled, "The American Movement," by Eugene V. Debs. It opens with the statement that "The twentieth century, according to the prophecy of Victor Hugo, is to be the century of humanity," and will witness "the crash of despotism and the rise of world-wide democracy, freedom and brotherhood." The reader, continuing, soon discovers that the "American movement," with which this pamphlet deals, is the American Socialist movement. The writer tells of its early "Utopian" forms, the Owenites and the Brook-farmers, and names the exiles who came from abroad in 1848, bringing the Marxian doctrine, and influencing such men as Horace Greeley and Parke Godwin. "The first large society to adopt and propagate Socialism in America," he writes, "was composed of the German Gymnastic Unions. Through the sixties and seventies the agitation steadily increased, local organisations were formed in various parts of the country. Following the Paris Commune of 1871, and its tragic ending, many French radicals came to our shores and gave new spirit to the movement. In 1876 the Workingman's Party was organised, and in 1877, at the convention held in Newark, it became the Socialist Labour Party. The Socialists were intent upon building up a working-class party for independent political action." This party, "composed of thoughtful, intelligent men, aggressive and progressive, of rugged honesty and thrilled with the revolutionary spirit and aspiration for freedom, became from its inception a decided factor in the labour movement. The busy, ignorant world about the revolutionary nucleus knew little or nothing about it; had no conception of its significance, and looked upon its adherents as foolish fanatics whose antics were harmless and whose designs would dissolve like bubbles on the surface of a stream. In March, 1885, was inaugurated the strike of the Knights of Labour. On May 1st of the same year, the general strikes for the eight-hour work-day broke out in various parts of the country. In 1884, Laurence Gronlund published his "Coöperative Commonwealth." In 1888 Edward Bellamy published his "Looking Backward," and it had a wonderful effect upon the people. The editions ran into hundreds of thousands."

The author then goes on to narrate his version of the Pullman strike of 1893. He declares that the American Railway Union, of which he was president, had won, when the General Managers' Association caused the swearing in of "an army of deputies," whom the Chief of Police of Chicago declared to be "thieves, thugs and ex-convicts," and that it was these men who caused the violence which led to President Cleveland's action, and the breaking of the strike. He then continues the story of the Socialist movement. *The Coming Nation*, started at Greensburg, Indiana, by J. A. Wayland, in 1893, was the first popular propaganda paper to be published in the interests of Socialism in this country. It reached a large circulation, and the proceeds were used in founding and developing the Ruskin coöperative colony in Tennessee. Later Mr. Wayland began the publication of the *Appeal to Reason*, and it now numbers its subscribers by the hundreds of thousands. It is not saying too much for the *Appeal* that it has been a great factor in preparing the American soil for the seed of Socialism. Its enormous editions have been and are being spread broadcast, and copies may be found in the remotest recesses and the most inaccessible regions. The periodical and weekly press, so necessary to any political movement, is now developing rapidly, and there is every reason to believe that within the next few years there will be a formidable array of reviews, magazines, illustrated journals, and daily and weekly papers to represent the movement and do battle for its supremacy. The last convention of the American Railway Union was the first convention of the Social Democracy of America, and this was held in Chicago, in June, 1897, the delegates voting to change the railway union into a working-class political party. *The Railway Times*, the official paper of the union, became the *Social-Democrat*, and later the *Social-Democratic Herald*, and is now published at Milwaukee in the interest of the Socialist Party. Since the election of 1900, there has been greater activity in organising, and a more widespread propaganda than ever before. In the elections of the past, it can scarcely be claimed that the Socialist movement was represented by a national party. It entered these contests with but few states organised, and with

The Coming Crisis

no resources worth mentioning to sustain it during the campaign. It is far different to-day. The Socialist Party is organised in almost every state and territory in the American Union. Its members are filled with enthusiasm and working with an energy born of the throb and thrill of revolution. The party has a press supporting it that extends from sea to sea, and is as vigilant and tireless in its labours as it is steadfast and true to the party principles.

"Viewed to-day from any intelligent standpoint, the outlook of the Socialist movement is full of promise—to the capitalist, of struggle and conquest; to the worker, of coming freedom. It is the break of dawn upon the horizon of human destiny, and it has no limitation but the walls of the universe."

Whatever the reader may think about the foregoing narrative, there is one part of it which he cannot dismiss; the statements concerning the growth of the American Socialist Party. In 1888 the Socialist vote was two thousand. In 1892, it was twenty-one thousand. In 1896, it was thirty-six thousand. In 1900, it was one hundred and thirty-one thousand. In 1904, it was four hundred and forty-two thousand.

The Socialist Party has some twenty-seven thousand subscribing members, who pay monthly dues. It has over eighteen hundred "locals," or centres of agitation; the members of these "locals" are for the most part workingmen, who give their spare hours to the cause, holding meetings and debates, and circulating the literature of Socialism. In the larger cities, there are generally several lectures each week, and there are a score of "national organisers," who travel about, speaking night after night in various towns, forming new "locals," and taking subscriptions to the Socialist publications. Of these there are four monthlies and about thirty-five weeklies. Since 1892, Wayland's paper, *The Appeal to Reason* (Girard, Kansas), has increased its paid circulation from one hundred and twenty-six thousand to over two hundred and seventy-five thousand, and last year it printed one edition of two millions and a half, and another of over three millions. Another Socialist paper, *Wilshire's Magazine* (New York), has increased its circulation from fifty-five thousand to two hundred and seventy thousand in a single year. In addition to this, there are many publishing companies, which distribute books, leaflets and pamphlets, at little more than cost. I have before me a treatise, the price of which is one cent, of which over five million copies have been sold since its publication some years ago. Its title is "Why Workingmen Should Be Socialists," by Gaylord Wilshire.

And in giving the figures of the Socialist growth, it is worth while to point out that this is not merely a local movement, but a world movement; that the United States is one of the most backward of the civilised nations in respect to Socialism. In Australia the labour unions have adopted a full Socialist program, and the labour unions hold the balance of power. In England, they have just elected twenty-seven members of Parliament; they have now members in the Cabinet of France, and in Italy they have turned out ministries. In Belgium, the vote of the party is half a million, and in Austria it is nearly a million, while in Germany it has grown from thirty thousand in 1870, to five hundred and forty-nine thousand in 1884, one million, eight hundred and seventy-six thousand in 1893, three million and eight thousand in 1903 and three million two hundred and fifty thousand in 1907. The Socialists are electing representatives in Argentina and South Africa; in spite of government persecution, the movement is now growing rapidly in Japan. Including all languages, the Socialist journals number nearly seven hundred, and the Socialist vote of the world is figured at nearly eight million. Allowing for women, and for the disfranchised proletariat of such nations as Russia, Austria, and Italy, there are estimated to be thirty million class-conscious Socialists in the world.

To overlook the significance of a movement such as this, is but to repeat upon a larger scale the error of half a century ago, and to pay with blood and anguish for blundering and indifference. The processes of time have their laws, which can be studied; and all the waste and ruin of history, which make its records scarcely to be read, are consequences of the fact that man has to be lashed to his goal through the darkness, instead of marching to it in the light. You take but a shallow view of the problems of our present time, if you do not realise that when thirty million people, in every corner of the civilised world, organise themselves into a political party, they do it because of some fundamental and tremendous motive, and that they will not be apt to abandon their efforts until they have accomplished some proportionately significant result.

CHAPTER II

INDUSTRIAL EVOLUTION

HERBERT SPENCER gives a definition of Evolution, phrased in technical terms, which might be roughly summed up in these words: A process whereby many similar and simple things become dissimilar parts of one complex thing. If we trace, for instance, the evolution of human society, we see about as follows: In the beginning man exists in widely scattered and unrelated tribes, having a very loosely organised government, each individual doing about as he pleases, and all individuals being very much the same. Each finds his own food and cooks it, makes his own weapons and clothing, and looks and thinks and acts like his neighbour. Little by little, as the tribe grows, it begins to come into contact with other tribes that also are growing, and a pressure begins; the tribes make war upon each other, and each individual of the tribe is forced by the presence of danger to unite himself more closely with his fellows, to establish a more rigid rule of obedience, and to force refractory members to the general will. Then, under still growing pressure, one tribe unites with another against a common enemy, and the strongest man in the two rules both; which process of combining continues until at last there results an organism of great complexity, whose members are no longer equal and self-sustaining, but have different activities and ranks and characteristics, and are each dependent upon the rest. If, for instance, we examine France during the Feudal period, we find numerous principalities, duchies and baronies, each one an elaborate and complex organisation, with various classes and hierarchies and tributary parts, and a whole system of laws and customs and beliefs to correspond. And no sooner is this process complete than an evolution begins among these organisms; under the stress of jealousies and ambitions they too begin to struggle, to combine; and presently in one of them arises a strong man who secures command of them all. When the process is completed, there stands in the place of a hundred principalities, one kingdom, the Kingdom of France.

The object of all this long labour is, of course, to get some kind of an organism that shall be capable of maintaining itself in a world of ferocious strife; that shall be able to withstand all enemies that may come against it, and all rebellions that may arise within it. The French monarchy was a marvellous piece of work when it was done; it had men graded into a thousand different classes and occupations, and everything fitted perfectly and ran like a clock. It had peasants to till the soil, and soldiers and sailors to fight; artisans to make all its necessaries, and merchants to handle them; and rising tier upon tier, a whole pyramid of governing and administrative officials, up to the king. It had likewise the whole outfit of ideas and customs necessary to its operation; it was complete and perfect and sublime—it was like a mighty vessel defying the tempests; it had also its pennons that waved, and its songs for the crew to sing. Was it any wonder that those who had made it were proud of it, and felt that there was nothing more to be done in the world but to keep it going?

And yet evolution was not through with it. Men grow weary and want to rest, they become "conservative" and fret at the bare thought of change—but the processes of life go on inexorably. This mighty structure, the Kingdom of France, was only a means and not an end—its purpose was to bind the people of the nation together and protect them until they were able to take care of themselves. It took a long time for this idea to make its way; it took a fearful struggle—men were imprisoned and exiled, burned and beheaded;

but the idea went right on, and the nation went right on; and when the time came, it burst the old integument to pieces, and out of the Kingdom of France there emerged the French Republic.

What a marvellous event that was, and what a stir it made in the world—what a stir especially in our own corner of the world—every one knows. Looking at it from a century's distance, and calmly, we see the whole age-long event as an exemplification of the process of life; the combining of a number of simple things into one complex thing. The means was struggle and rivalry—it was a cruel process; but you will notice that at the end the effort and the pain are all gone—that the organism fulfils its functions freely and joyfully, and that the only difference between the first stage and the last is that the individual man has been raised to a higher plane of being.

Now, as I have said before, the first care of a man is to protect his life; the second is to accumulate wealth. A man does not set much store by his goods while his enemies are within sound; but just as soon as they are dispersed, the tribe begins to gather flocks, and to till the soil. And so, following close upon the heels of the evolution of political society, you have the evolution of *industrial* society.

Industrial Evolution 31

And it is precisely the same process. We may see nearly the whole of it in this country. It begins with the colonial village, where every man owns a little land and raises his own food; also he cobbles his own shoes, spins his own wool, weaves his own cloth, and makes his own clothes. In the very earliest days, he never buys anything, because there is nothing to buy. He may be the deacon or the schoolmaster or the judge, but still he has his own farm, and any other man in the village is about as well fitted to be the deacon or the school-master or the judge as he. But then his goods expand and war begins—industrial war, I mean—a horse-trade, for example. Political evolution is slow, because the rate of increase of men is limited; but the rate of increase of goods proves to be unlimited. Machines are invented, and straightway the industrial process is accelerated tenfold. It took a thousand years to evolve a monarchy; it took only a hundred to evolve a trust.

The industrial units fight each other, and the strongest survive as employers, the weakest becoming employees. Then, as growth continues, these various little groups all over the country come into contact, and they struggle also. The struggle is of course no longer fighting with swords—it is underselling; but the process is exactly the same, and its purpose is the building up of a capable industrial organism. Precisely as in one case the tribes by combining find they are stronger to fight, the employers, by combining, find that they are stronger to undersell; and this process goes on until you have an industrial feudalism, corresponding in all its details to the political feudalism of France. And then, as before, the barons and the princes and the dukes fight among each other, until out of the midst arises a strong man, a Rockefeller or a Harriman, who smashes them right and left, and makes himself a king.

He is a king in precisely the same way, and to precisely the same purpose, as Louis the Great was king. You know how Richelieu served the nobility of France—if they would not obey they simply lost their heads. If you have read Miss Tarbell's "History of the Standard Oil Company," or Henry D. Lloyd's "Wealth Against Commonwealth," you know how Mr. Rockefeller served the oil nobility; how he tricked them and crushed them; how sometimes, it is said, he blew up their refineries with dynamite, or burned them with fire. You know how Louis said he was the State; and you heard the president of one of the coal companies, who is doing business in flat defiance of the laws of the land, declare that God in His Infinite Wisdom had en-

Industrial Evolution

trusted to him the property interests of the country. It is not necessary to pursue this analogy; if you do not see that in the due and inevitable course of evolution, our industrial organism has attained the monarchical stage, it is simply because you do not wish to see it, and no amount of exposition will avail. I have only to add, as before, that the purpose of *this* process was to evolve an organism which should be capable of maintaining itself against all enemies, without and within. The task of King Louis was the aggrandisement of France; the task of Mr. Rockefeller is the keeping up of Standard Oil stock. Incidentally, Louis the Great gave the world a race-heritage and a civilisation; incidentally, Mr. Rockefeller furnishes the world with oil. Also—what is true in one case is true in the other—the Standard Oil Company is a marvellous piece of work. It has men graded into a thousand different classes and occupations, and all fitting perfectly and running like a clock. It has labourers to till the soil, lobbyists and salesmen to fight, factories to make all its necessaries, and railroads to handle them; and, rising tier upon tier, it has a whole pyramid of governing and administrative officials, up to the president. It has likewise the whole outfit of ideas necessary to its operation; it is complete and perfect and sublime—it is like a mighty vessel, defying the tempests. Is it any wonder that those who have constructed it are proud of it, and feel that there is nothing more to be done in the world but to keep it going?

It is of course clear that the next step, according to my parallel, would be into an Industrial Republic. The reader differs from most Americans whom I meet if this idea is not startling to him. Let us go forward slowly.

In Mr. John Bach McMaster's "History of the People of the United States," is a narrative of the terrible yellow-fever epidemic which occurred in Philadelphia in the year 1793, causing the death of over four thousand people in four months. In those days men had strange ideas as to the causes of yellow fever; they believed, in this case, that it "had come from a pile of stinking hides that had been on one of the wharves." The historian goes on to describe the strange expedients they adopted to get rid of it. "People were bidden to keep out of the sun, and not to get tired. The doctors had little faith in bonfires as purifiers of the air, but much in the burning of gunpowder. Every one then who could buy or borrow a gun, loaded and fired it from morning till night. Then one remedy after another would be suggested, and people would cover themselves with it—nitre, to-

Industrial Evolution 35

tobacco, and garlic, mud-baths, camphor, and thieves' vinegar. The last could only be be procured by going to the shop. The purchaser going to get it was careful to have a piece of tarred rope wet with camphor at his nose, and in his pocket his handkerchief soaked with the last preventive he had heard of. He shunned the footpaths, fled down the nearest alley at sight of a carriage, and would go six blocks to avoid passing a house where a dead body had been taken out a week before. He would not enter a shop where another man stood at the counter; he would rush in, throw down the money, and rush home—soak everything in this prepared vinegar, and live on a prescribed diet, water-gruel, oatmeal, tea, barley-water, or a vile concoction called apple-tea. If his head pained him or his tongue felt rough, he would immediately wash out his mouth with warm water and honey and vinegar——" etc., etc. At the time when I read all this, it made a peculiar impression upon me, because the newspapers happened just then to be full of the discovery of the true cause of yellow fever. And so all the time that I was reading about the man with the tarred rope in his hands and a sponge wet with camphor at his nose, I had this thought in my mind: And while he was waiting outside of the shop, a mosquito flew up, all unheeded, and bit him. And so he died!

It seemed to me a peculiarly neat illustration of the precise difference between knowledge and ignorance. It led me to reflect how very eager men ought to be to possess the former; and I put the anecdote away in my mind, thinking, "I shall use it some day when I want—all of a sudden—to scare someone out of a prejudice!"

For just imagine, if you can, that mosquitoes, instead of being a pest about which every man was glad to believe evil, had been the basis of some important industry, or otherwise the source of incalculable advantage to the dominant classes of the community; that universities were endowed, and newspapers owned, and churches and hospitals supported, out of the proceeds of the mosquito monopoly! Are you sure that in that case the discovery of the physicians in Havana would have been hailed as a triumph of Science? Or do you not think that there might have been a strong opposition to the fantastic speculation, and that the men who had published it might have been denounced as enemies of society, and turned out of office for their incendiary teachings? That other physicians of high standing might have been found to ridicule the idea? That news-

Industrial Evolution

papers might have refused to print arguments in favour of it—that, in short, the mosquito monopoly might have succeeded in conjuring up before the imaginations of the multitude so horrible an image of this doctrine and its consequences, that they would have looked upon anyone who advocated it as in some way morally deformed? Assuming that this could have been done, there are only two things to be added. The first is that all the while the mosquitoes would have gone right on causing the yellow fever; and the second is that the people would have found it out in the end—that all that the makers of public opinion would have done, would be to put just so many millions of dollars into the pockets of the mosquito monopoly, at a cost of just so much misery to the human race.

At the outset of this argument, I very much wish that you, the reader, would commune with yourself prayerfully, as to whether or not it might not possibly be that the ideas you have in your head concerning an "Industrial Republic" are really not ideas of your own at all, but prejudices which other people have put there for purposes known to them.

Let me repeat the definition which I gave at the outset of this argument: I mean by an Industrial Republic, an organisation for the production of wealth, whose members are established upon a basis of equality; who elect representatives to govern the organisation; and who share equally in all its advantages.

A century or two ago our ancestors were governed, "by grace of God," by an unamiable old gentleman over in England, who controlled their destinies, and sent his representatives over here to tax and oppress them; and they impiously rose up and adopted a declaration to the effect that all men were born free and equal; and they seized the property and revenues of their king, and thereafter managed the country for their own benefit solely. "No taxation without representation," had been their doctrine beforehand. And you, who are an American, and celebrate the Fourth of July, and teach your children to admire the men who threw the tea into Boston Harbour—do you think that you could give me any reason why a man has a right to be represented where he pays his taxes, and no right to be represented where he gets his daily bread? Do you not perceive that a man who can say to me, "Do thus, or you and your children can have nothing to eat," is just as much my lord and master as the man who can say to me, "Do thus, or be put into jail?"

You stop and think. "The case is not

Industrial Evolution

quite the same," you say. "One is not represented, to be sure; but certainly every man has a right to get his daily bread as he pleases."

Indeed, I answer. Suppose, for instance, that his occupation happens to be that of a steel-worker; has he any way of getting his daily bread, except upon certain precise terms which a certain group of men offer him?

"H'm," you say, "that's so. But then, if he doesn't like it, can't he change his occupation?"

My answer is, I do not believe that George the Third would have had any objection to one of our ancestors going to France to become a subject of King Louis. But I understand that freedom began in America when the men of Lexington and Bunker Hill resolved to *stay at home* and be free.

"This is all very well in theory," you say, "but how can it ever be realised?" As I said before, I expect to see it realised in the United States of America within the next ten years. I expect to see it, exactly as I should have expected to see the French Revolution, had I known what I know now; understood that institutions and systems have their day, and perceived the signs of a breakdown as they existed in France in 1780, and as they exist in America in 1907.

What was the cause of the French Revolution? The French monarchy was organised upon a basis of force, represented by taxes; and those who ran the machine had no idea but that a machine so organised could go on forever. But in the long process of time, there developed a tendency on the part of those to whom the taxes came, to grow richer and richer, while those by whom the taxes were paid grew poorer and poorer. Little by little, all the property and all the land of France came into the hands of the nobility; until at last they had everything, and the populace had nothing. Then suddenly the machinery of a society organised upon a basis of force and taxes began to refuse to work; the French peasantry had stood everything, but they could not stand being required to pay taxes when they had nothing to pay with. So the States-General had to be sent for, and the Revolution came.

And note this—that the trouble was not at all that the country was poor. Everyone is familiar with the picture of the horrible condition of the peasantry of that time, how they were little better than wild animals, hiding in holes, naked, and with blackened skins. Yet all the while France was full of wealth—all the trouble was that it was stagnant in the hands of a single class; the fields of France were ready to produce, but the people were too poor to till them. And notice the curious fact, that no sooner was the Revolution accomplished than the difficulty vanished in a flash. The machinery started up again—the peasant had land and tilled it, and the artisans of the cities found work. It seems strange to read that under the "Terror," when the heads of the "aristocrats" were falling by the dozens every day and all the world was convulsed with horror, the *people* of France were more prosperous and happy than ever they had been before in history. And when war broke out, the nation that had been on the verge of bankruptcy for a generation, withstood the armies of the combined kingdoms of Europe for more than twenty years!

Here in America, we all started even. Wages were high, and there was work for every man; there was no need to strike—a workingman had only to leave and go elsewhere if he were not pleased. We found employment for the stream of immigrants as fast as they came—we had an enormous country to build up, and an inexhaustible supply of new lands for the settler. We manufactured only for our own use, and we could not manufacture half of what we needed.

But time passed on. Some who were frugal and diligent—and others who were cunning and unscrupulous—grew rich; and then machinery came in, and the pace grew faster. The rich were on top, and they stayed there. As the country expanded, railroads were built, and fortunes made; the war came, with its enormous expenditures, and still more fortunes were made. Capital grew; but it could not grow fast enough—in the seventies the rate of interest was ten per cent., and the promoters made fortunes besides. It was in those days that the battles of the giants were fought, the railroad wars in which the Gould and Vanderbilt millions were accumulated. Still there was plenty to do; the people had money, and there were some of them to buy everything we could make, and what came from abroad besides. The cities grew and spread, and the immigrants flowed in; railroads and factories were built, and the mighty structure of our modern industrial machine began to take shape. It must be understood that all the while inventions and improvements were being made, that enabled one man to do the work of ten, of fifty, of a hundred; and each such improvement set free so many thousands more men, to turn their attention to another part of the structure and to rush it on to completion.

Completion! Has it never dawned upon you that this machine might possibly some day reach completion?

The purpose of it is a very definite and

Industrial Evolution

obvious one—it is to supply the needs of men; and when it is adequate to that purpose, it is complete. But how will you know when *that* is? Why, by the simplest of methods in the world—by that insufficiency of profits which I described before. You are in business for profits, you understand; and when you are making something that men need, you make profits; and when you are making something that men do not need, you *stop* making profits. It would be too bad if men went on making railroads where no one wanted to ride, and building houses for no one to occupy; how fortunate that Nature has arranged it so that we all know when our work is done!

We were trembling on the very verge—in fact, we were half-way over the verge—three years ago, when the Russo-Japanese War came along and saved us. Everybody had begun to realise the peril. The investor, who had been making ten per cent. in the seventies, came down to three. The workingman who had a job that did not suit him, stuck to it all the same, because he saw a million men in the country who had no job at all. And the capitalist, the captain of industry—he mounted into his watch-tower, and proceeded to scan the landscape. A market! A market! My kingdom for a market!

Our newspapers a few years ago were

quite wild with delight over a phenomenon called the "American Invasion." They told how we were conquering all over the world—how Europe stood shuddering with fright—how our exports were mounting by leaps and bounds! How prosperous we were! What ocean-tides of wealth were coming in to us! It seemed so strange to read it all, and to understand that this "Invasion" which the editors were celebrating, was in reality the last death-kick of the industrial system which they had been taught to consider the foundation of all society!

It will be more convenient to consider the whole question of foreign markets at a later stage; suffice it here to say, that if my analysis of the over-production of capital be correct, then the first signal of danger will be what is commonly hailed as a "favourable balance of trade"—the existence of a surplus product which must be sold abroad. You must distinguish, of course, between a mere exchange of goods, where exports are balanced by imports, and *selling*, which is sending out goods and taking in gold, or promises to pay gold. In 1893 our exports were eight hundred and forty-seven million dollars and our imports were eight hundred and sixty-six millions. But in 1901, our exports had leaped to one billion, four hundred and eighty-seven mil-

Industrial Evolution

lion dollars, and our imports had sunk to eight hundred and twenty-three millions; and during the next four years the excess of exports over imports amounted to a total of over a billion and a half of dollars! According to an estimate made public on January 6, 1907, by the Secretary of the Treasury, the figures for 1906 will be: Imports, one billion, two hundred million dollars, and exports, one billion, eight hundred million dollars. And for how many more years does anyone imagine that the world will be able to pay us six hundred million dollars in cash, for those surplus products which we are compelled to sell?

Do not fail to mark the word "compelled." If we cannot sell them, we cannot make profits; and if we cannot make profits, we cannot pay dividends. "I am a great clamourer for dividends," said Mr. Rockefeller; and other captains of industry share in his weakness. And when a few years ago they found that foreign markets were beginning to fail, they set to work to remedy the evil in the only other possible way—by combining, and limiting the product, and raising prices. And that brings us to the other great symptom of the approach of the breakdown—the organising of the trusts. For six or eight years the process has been going on, irresistibly, automatically—while the country raged and stormed, and poured out its wrath upon the greedy capitalist. And yet the capitalist was no more to blame than a steam-engine that turns aside when it comes to a switch. The capitalist was making profits; and he saw, by the cessation of his profits, that the industrial machine of the country was getting too big for the country's use. Unless he, and the machine also, were to go to smash, competition in that particular industry must be ended.

The work is done now; we have only to sit by and wait until the people get through trying to undo it. I never realise more keenly the naïve and touching incompetence of our so-called intellectual classes, than when I reflect that while our men of action have been accomplishing this mighty work —one of the greatest labours ever wrought for civilisation—our benevolent editors and college presidents have gone right on with their prattling of "freedom of contract" and "*laissez faire.*" And actually, civilisation must sit by and wait ten years, until our people have got through butting their heads against the granite wall of this accomplished fact!

But we Socialists have to take the world as we find it, and cultivate a cheerful disposition; and so behold our great national spectacle, the morality-play of the terrible hundred-headed monster of Competition!

Industrial Evolution

The terrible monster has killed and destroyed himself, according to the nature of him; but now by Congressional statute and Supreme Court decree he has been patched together again, and will be compelled to go on fighting! Or at least he shall be stuffed and mounted, and shall look as if he were fighting! He shall have wires attached to his joints and electric lights to gleam from his eyes; he shall be taken out in the gorgeous Presidential campaign chariot, drawn by the Grand Old Party elephant, and all the people shall see him, and marvel at his ferocity, and at the deadly conflict he wages among his various heads! Come now, O people!—come editors and statesmen and judges and bishops—come and see how the terrible hundred-headed monster rends and tears himself, and shout for four years more of the "full dinner-pail."

But surely we must destroy the trusts! you say. *Why* must we destroy the trusts? The trusts are marvellous industrial machines, of power the like of which was never known in the world before; they are the last and most wonderful of the products of civilisation—and we must destroy them! We have been a century building them— you, and I, and the balance of the American people have toiled for three generations night and day, stinting and starving ourselves, so that we might get these trusts finished; we have taxed ourselves ten, twenty, thirty per cent. of our incomes, under the disguise of a protective tariff, to maintain and develop them; and now that they are complete, we must destroy them!

But they belong to Rockefeller! you protest to me. They belong to Rockefeller in precisely the same way and to precisely the same extent as the Kingdom of France belonged to Louis XIV, or the North American colonies to George III. They belong to the people of the United States, who made them, who contributed every plank of them, and drove every nail of them, and who paid Mr. Rockefeller and his family ample living wages while they superintended the job.

But you only answer again—we must destroy the trusts! Go ahead then, and have your try! Have it out with them! War to the hilt with them!—and see which is the stronger, two corporations which are resolved not to cut each other's throats, or you with your law that they *shall* cut each other's throats! Two railroad systems which know that they cannot continue to exist separately, or you who are resolved that they shall not exist together!—It makes one think of the scene in "Twelfth Night," where Sir Toby has engineered a bloody duel between two terror-stricken antagonists. "Pox on't, I'll not meddle with him!" cries

A SOCIALIST VIEW OF THE TRUSTS

Sir Andrew Aguecheek. "Come, Sir Andrew," says Sir Toby. "There's no remedy. Come on, to't." But poor Sir Andrew will not to't, he fights with his back to the enemy.

You will hear people abuse the Socialists for wishing to abolish competition. No Socialist wishes to abolish competition, no modern Socialist at any rate. He watches competition, as the mischievous Irishmen watched the Kilkenny cats; keeping off at a suitable distance during the battle, and simply proposing to the spectators that when it is all over they shall recognise the accomplished fact.

There is some competition in the world to-day among the nations; there was recently competition between Russia and Japan, and there will perhaps be competition between some of the others. But what competition is left to-day within the limits of the United States, is left simply because it is of a kind so petty that the capitalists have not yet had time to bother with it. For the most part it exists between a swarm of retailers of trust-made products, and takes the form of the screwing down of the wages of helpless clerks and errand-boys, the adulteration of products, and the placarding of the surface of the land with blatant advertisements which affect a decent man like the stench of a carcass. One of the "competitive" industries that is flourishing just now is that of cereals prepared in packages and labelled with names that suggest Hiawatha and the South Sea Islands. The usual price of one of these packages is fifteen cents, and of that, two cents and a half represents the cost of the product, and nearly all of the balance goes into the effort to trap the public into buying it. And did not the "boodle" investigations in Missouri disclose the fact that William Ziegler had spent a fortune in bribing newspapers and legislatures to implant in the public mind the idea that "alum baking-powders" were poisonous, so that the Royal Baking Powder Trust might have the custom of the country?

But, you say, if competition perishes, what becomes of incentive—of initiative? Will not individual enterprise be destroyed? I answer that it depends entirely upon what you mean by individual enterprise. If you mean that ardent desire which now consumes every man to cut his neighbour's economic throat, to get the better of him and make money out of him, to beat him down and leave him a financial wreck—why, civilisation will suppress this ardent desire in precisely the same way that it has suppressed the duel, or the right of private vengeance, and piracy, or the right of private war upon the high seas. The putting down of these things went hard, you know, for they had been the greatest glory of men, and all progress has been due to them. "Franz von Sickingen was a robber-knight," writes Henderson, in his "History of Germany," "but with such noble traits, and such a concept of his calling, that one wonders if he ought not rather to be put on the level of a belligerent prince. In carrying on feuds, he seldom aimed lower than a duke, or a free city of the Empire; and there are persons who insist to this day that his weapons were only drawn in favour of the oppressed. Be that as it may, he was not above exacting enormous fines; and being an excellent manager, he greatly increased his possessions. He was lord of many castles, which he furnished with splendid defences."

And then the historian goes on to describe the gallant struggle of this old nobleman against the advancing power of the Empire. "He determined, by one brilliant-feud, to restore the tarnished splendour of his name. He would help the whole order of knighthood to assert itself against the power of the princes." The end of it was that "the enemy appeared in full force, demolished in a single day an outer tower with walls the thickness of twenty feet, and made a breach in the actual ramparts."

Having been wounded, "the grim commander was carried to a dark, deep vault of the castle, where it was thought he would be safe from the cannon-balls of his pursuers; such an unchristian shooting, he declared to an attendant, he had never heard in all his days." The castle surrendered, and his foes gathered about him. "He had now to do, he said, with a greater lord, and a few hours later he closed his eyes. The three princes knelt at his side and prayed God for the peace of his soul." Let us hope that the makers of our Industrial Republic will not forget to pray for the souls of Baer and Parry, if these gallant captains of industry should perish in defending the elemental right of a capitalist to manage his own business in his own way.

This is all very well, you say, but will not such a system decrease production? I rather think that it will; I hope to see the prophecy of Annie Besant come true, that when men no longer have to struggle to get a living, they will at last begin to live. That they will at last open their eyes to the world of books and music, of nature and art, of friendship and love, that stretches out its arms to them; that they will cease to regard ingenuity and rapidity in the production of material things as the final end and goal of the creation of man; that they will cease to look upon a human being as a

Industrial Evolution 53

machine for the getting of money—to be valued like an automobile, by the number of miles an hour it can be driven, by the number of thousands of miles it can cover before it is worn out and ready for the scrap-heap.

Let us have the philosophy of this thing, in order that we may understand it. We saw that the process of evolution, in an individual or in a society, consists of an expansion and a struggle, the end of which is the emergence of the organism into a higher state of being. There is a certain life impulse, and there is a certain environment, certain difficulties with which it contends. We have perhaps no right to speak of purpose in the process, but we have a right to speak of results; and the result of this contest is to shape the organism, to educate it, to bring out certain qualities in it which it did not possess before; until finally it triumphs over its environment, and emerges from its prison-house.

The struggle for life goes on, but the form of it changes unceasingly; and this changing is *progress*. Without it there can be none—the very essence of progress consists in the suppressing of old forms of strife, the conquest of old difficulties and the escape from their thraldom. We know that there was once a time when men were hairy beings who dwelt in caves, and contended with club and hatchet against the monsters which assailed them; and now supposing that we could take some man of modern times, some one who has risen to eminence and power under the conditions which now prevail, and put him among those cave-men, how do you suppose that he would make out? How do you suppose that he would fare, if he were placed even one century back, in the country of the Iroquois, where the snapping of a twig and the flight of an arrow decided the fate of a man? Is it not obvious that there has been here an entire change in the *form* of the struggle for existence?

The same thing is true of nations. Once upon a time a nation was an army, and fighting was its business, the conquering of its neighbours was its glory and its ideal; but now we have moved on, we have become complex and highly organised, and can no longer afford to conquer our neighbours. It would not pay us financially, and intellectually and morally it would destroy us. We have, for instance, a powerful country to the north of us; and imagine what would be the inconvenience and waste were we under the necessity of fortifying all our boundary lines, and keeping garrisons at every few miles of them; if every day we were shaken by rumours that an army was gathering at Montreal, that a fleet of torpedo-boats was building at Toronto. As a matter of simple fact, do we not both go quietly on our way, understanding that we are two civilised nations, between which a war of conquest would be an unthinkable crime?

We have grown so used to the change, that the mere memory of the old ways of life makes us shudder; it seems to us horrible, and we forget that it was once beautiful and delightful to men: that the Germans of the time of Tacitus held fighting the joy of life, and imagined a heaven where a man might be patched up every night and fight again the next day. We have passed so far beyond such a state that we cannot even imagine it, and we have lost the power of seeing that it was ever necessary and right; that to those long ages of struggle we owe our physical being, with all its perfections, which we take so as a matter of course; a swift foot and a dexterous hand, an ear attuned to every sound, an eye that adjusts itself to every distance, a mind quick and alert, a spirit bold and enterprising. And in the same way the nations owe to war their unity and their complexity, and a great deal of their power, not merely physical, but industrial and moral as well.

It was one of the noblest of the world's poets who wrote that:

> "God's most dreaded instrument,
> In working out a pure intent,
> Is man—arrayed for mutual slaughter;
> Yea, Carnage is His daughter."

And to the same purpose writes Fletcher:

> "Oh great corrector of enormous times,
> Shaker of o'er-rank states—that
>   heal'st with blood
> The earth when it is sick."

And yet the time of wars is past. We still have them, of course, and we still have a war-propaganda; but it would be easy to show that these wars are never military, but always commercial—that when two civilised states fight nowadays, it is not because they expect to subjugate each other, or desire to, but because their capitalists both need the same foreign market. I am acquainted with only one writer of any standing in the United States, Captain Mahan, who is nowadays willing even to hint that wars may still be necessary to the disciplining of a nation; and I think one might assert without fear of contradiction that people now go to war, not because they want to, but because they are persuaded they have to; and that right-thinking men throughout the world know that a war is a national calamity, a cause of evils innumerable, scarcely ever overbalanced by good.

Industrial Evolution

And it is of the utmost importance to notice how this has been done; how it is that the military ideal is universally discredited in the world. It has not been due to the preachings of moralists and enthusiasts; it has not been brought about by the intervention of any *deus ex machina*. It has come about in the perfectly inevitable course of nature. No hero has arisen to slay the demon of war—the demon of war has slain himself. It is simply that the work of war is *done*. It is simply that war has brought about a survival of the fittest, and that there is no more need of conquest, and no possibility of it. The peoples have gone on to a different life, they have almost forgotten for thought of conquering, or of being conquered; they know that they cannot afford it; they know that their social organism is of too delicate a type to stand it; they can no more stand it than one of our modern captains of industry could stand the shock of jousting with Richard Cœur de Lion.

We have moved on to another kind of struggle—to the kind which is known as industrial competition. And we are to come to the end of that in precisely the same way. We are to see the fittest survive, and grow, and establish themselves impregnably; and so long as there is room for competition they will compete; and when they find there is no longer room for competition, that by continuing it they are doing as much harm to themselves as to their rivals, they will put an end to competition, and no power on earth can prevent their putting an end to it. Any power which really tried to prevent their putting an end to it would simply destroy them, as two civilised nations would be destroyed if they could be compelled to keep on making war against each other.

The great task of civilisation is the leading of men to recognise when these mighty changes have taken place. For so far I have spoken of only one side of the evolutionary process; I have shown the victory—but there are also defeats. Sometimes in the struggle between the individual and his environment, it is the environment that conquers. Sometimes the man or the society is not equal to the new task, and falls back; and the law of this is death. The stag which can run swiftly enough escapes, and is able to run all the more swiftly as the result of the race; the stag which cannot run quite swiftly enough becomes venison. The tiny shoot which can grow high enough finds the light, and becomes a mighty tree; its neighbour which could not grow quite so high, turns to mould. There comes now and then in the history of every living thing some moment when its

Industrial Evolution 59

future hangs in the balance; when it summons all its forces, and lives or dies. The butterfly faces such a crisis when it emerges from the chrysalis; the child when it is born. You have known such fateful hours in your own moral life; and you can go through history and put your finger upon them—here when the Greeks drove back the Persians, here when the Franks drove back the Saracens, here on the field of Waterloo, on the hills of Gettysburg.

You would like to stay as you are, of course; for that is the least trouble. You have your routine and your habits, your old well-worn paths in which your thoughts move—you would like to stay as you are. But the curse of life is upon you—you cannot stay as you are. You have to go forward, or else to go back. When the crisis comes there is no escaping it—it *comes*. When the birth-pangs begin, either the child is born, or the mother dies; when the throes of revolution seize a nation, either the old forms are shattered, or the life of the people is crushed. There was once a reformation and a revolution in France; there was no reformation and no revolution in Spain. So in one case you have new life and abounding vigour—literatures and philosophies and sciences, and impulse after impulse without end; and on the other hand you have stagnation and ruin.

The task was simply too hard for the Spanish nation; they had lived for centuries in imminent proximity to an enemy of an alien faith, and the result was the fastening upon the people of a system of military despotism and religious bigotry. And when the danger was by, when the work of these forces was done, and the time came for the people of Spain to throw them off, their efforts were of no avail; their kings and their priests tortured them and burned them at the stake; and so the impulse died, and never afterwards did they lift their heads. In the same way consider the "Negro question," as we have it in the United States. Here also we are dealing with a defeated race; a race which was bred where nature proved too strong for man—where savage beasts fell upon him, and deadly diseases smote him, and the swift powers of the jungle balked his every effort to rise. So for centuries and ages he was trampled upon and crushed, until every spark of genius was extinguished in him; and now we strive with all the resources of our civilisation—our noblest and best have given their lives to the task; and we do not know yet if we are to win or lose.

Let the reader of this book get a clear understanding upon at least one point—that no Socialist expects to abolish competition, and the survival of the fittest; all

Industrial Evolution 61

that any Socialist expects to do is to change the *kind* of competition and the standard of the fitness. The purpose of industrial competition is to raise up the industrially fit, and to establish a system for the feeding and clothing of men. The sign that the former task is done is the outcry against the money-madness of the time; the sign that the latter is done is "overproduction" and the "trust."

The purpose of this little book is to lay before candid and truth-seeking Americans the overwhelming evidence which exists of the fact that industrial competition, as an evolutionary force, has done its work in our society: that it has disciplined our labourers in diligence and skill, and our leaders in foresight, enterprise and administrative capacity; that it has built us up a machine for the satisfying of all the material needs of civilisation, a machine that has only to be used; and that until we have found out how to use it, our national life must remain at a standstill, stagnation must take the place of progress, and in every portion of our body politic, the symptoms of disease and decay must multiply and grow more and more alarming.

We have been taught to think that the institutions of freedom in this country are so secure that we may go about our business and our play, and leave them to take care of themselves. And yet, "eternal vigilance is the price of liberty," is the motto our ancestors left us. For the forms of tyranny change from generation to generation, and it is always out of the old freedom that the new slavery is made. You think that you can stay free by clinging to the good old ways, by repeating the good old formulas, by standing by the good old faiths; but you cannot, for freedom is not a thing of institutions, but of the soul. It has always been under the forms of spirituality that men have been chained by priestcraft; and it is with the very pennons and banners of liberty that this land is bound to-day. It always has been so, and it always will be so—that the despot asks nothing save that things should stay as they are. What was it that the slave-holder wanted, but that things should stay as they were? That men should hold by the Constitution as it was, while America was made into a Slave Empire? What is it that our masters want to-day, save that we should stand by the good old traditions of American individualism, freedom of contract and the right of every man to manage his own business as he pleases—the while the Republic of Jefferson and Lincoln is forged into a weapon for the enslaving of mankind?

There is not one single tradition of the early times that is not being used to-day

Industrial Evolution 63

for the betraying of liberty. Take the Monroe Doctrine, for instance. We shout for it every Fourth of July, and we are rushing to completion a score or two of battleships to defend it; whenever it is in peril, our most rabid anti-trust editors and politicians drop everything and take to singing Yankee Doodle. And yet, has never the least suspicion about it come to you? Has it never occurred to you to look who it is that is leading you upon this crusade of freedom—this strange propaganda of civilisation and republican institutions by battleship and rapid-firing gun? This zeal of our captains of industry for the spread of American institutions among the Filipinos and Hawaiians and Porto Ricans and Panamanians and Venezuelans, the while they are so busy crushing American institutions in Rhode Island and Colorado!

There was once a time when all the despotisms of Europe were banded together to destroy republican institutions, and when the threatening gesture of this young republic held them back from half a world. And thus bravely we guarded civilisation with our Monroe Doctrine, until the lesson of freedom had been learned. But now time has passed, and we have come to a new age, with new perils and new duties; there is a new kind of slavery in the world, and a kind in which we lead all civilisation.

The control of our Republic has passed out of the hands of the people; by fraud and force our liberties have been overthrown —the very word has been relegated to schoolboy orations and Grand Army reunions. And by this new despotism of greed the people have first been plundered and crushed, and now are to be marshalled and led out to do battle with other peoples, similarly beguiled. In this work every force of reaction and conservatism in civilised society is now enlisted, every tradition of olden time has been called into service. No pretence is too hollow, no blasphemy too abominable to be employed; every national prejudice, every racial hatred, every religious bigotry is made use of—and the starving wretches of the slums and gutters of London are sent into South Africa to capture diamond mines for the glory of free Britannia, while the helpless peasants of Russia are led out with jewelled images of the Virgin in front of them to steal Manchuria in the name of Jesus Christ.

It is with Germany that we Americans are scheduled to battle for the sake of the Monroe Doctrine. And what is the situation in Germany? There is first of all, the degenerate who sits upon its throne, and proclaims himself by grace of God the lord and master of the German people. There is in the second place, the hide-bound

Industrial Evolution   65

mediæval nobility of the Empire, the direct descendants of those robber-knights of whom we read a while ago, some of them living in the very same castles from which their ancestors made their raids. There is in the third place, the aristocracy of the army, whose insolent and dissolute officers beat, kick and maim the helpless country boys and artisans who are herded like sheep under their command. There is in the fourth place, the bigoted seventeenth-century Protestant Church, with its snuffy country parsons and doctors of dusty divinity. There is in the fifth place, the mediæval Roman Catholic Church, with its confessional and other agencies of Darkness. There is in the sixth place, a subsidised "reptile press," whose opinions are written and whose news is garbled by knavish bureau officials. And every one of these powers, forgetting all past differences, and uniting with brotherly affection, are struggling with every prejudice they can appeal to, and every threat which they can wield, to hold the German people subject to the identical same "System" that rules in America, the industrial aristocracy of cunning and greed; is working them upon starvation wages at home, and driving them to serve in armies and navies, to conquer markets abroad; to threaten Dewey at Manila, and to seize Chinese ports and conduct "punitive expeditions" against Chinamen; to sell bad whiskey and firearms to Hereros and then slaughter them when they rebel; to blockade ports in Venezuela and to sink "pirates" in the West Indies; and to sound and measure channels as a preliminary to the taking of a naval base and the inauguration of a war with the United States!

But then, you say, *we* can't help that. What can we *do?* Is the only thing you can think of to do, to build battleships and get ready for the strife? How differently our fathers did it, in the old days when the Monroe Doctrine was really what it pretends to be—a pledge of freedom to men! How the impulses that started in this land thrilled through the civilised world and made the "despots of Europe" tremble! What messages of brotherhood flashed upon invisible wires from continent to continent, bearing hope and comfort to all the oppressed of mankind! How we welcomed Lafayette, as if he had been an emperor! How the whole nation turned out in honour of Kossuth, making his long journey one triumphal procession! And are we doing anything like that now?

The people of Germany, you must understand, are closed in a death grip with all these powers of infamy. In spite of obloquy and contempt, in spite of lies and blandishments and menaces, in spite of persecution and exile and imprisonment, for a generation they have been toiling—devoted, heroic men and women have given their labour and their lives to the task of teaching, writing, speaking, exhorting, to open the eyes of the masses to the truth. And step by step they have marched on, gathering force every hour, strengthened by each new persecution, training themselves in literary and political combat, building up a system of scientific thought which has never been refuted and never can be, inspired by a moral purpose as noble as any the world has ever seen—preparing in all ways for the glorious hour when the people of the Fatherland are to come to their own! The man at their head was once a poor working boy, a wheelwright, and he has raised himself to the leadership of the mightiest effort after freedom that the world now sees; and day by day in the Reichstag he leads the opposition to militarism and savagery, and his speeches are such as a century ago, and even half a century ago, would have set this land aflame from end to end with revolutionary fervour. And this is no isolated movement of a nation, it is a world movement—it is a movement to which the lovers of liberty all over the earth are welcomed as comrades and brothers. It is a movement at one with every high tradition of American life; and you—what is your attitude to it? What do you know about it—what do you care about it? Do you hold public meetings and send messages of sympathy? Do the halls of Congress ring with fervid speeches, as they did in the days of Webster and Henry Clay? Do your papers teem with glowing editorials, with news about the movement, and sketches of its leaders? What have you to say about it, what have you to do for it—but to repeat day in and day out one miserable, pitiful lie, with which you try to blind and deceive the masses of your own country, that this tremendous Socialist movement is not really a Socialist movement at all, but only a movement of political reform!

I do not think that we shall sleep forever; I do not think that the memories of Jefferson and Lincoln will call to us in vain forever; but assuredly there never was in all American history a sign of torpor so deep, of degeneration so frightful, as this fact that in such a crisis, when the downtrodden millions of the German Empire are struggling to free themselves from the tyranny of military and personal government, there should come to them not one breath of sympathy from the people of the American Republic! And all our interest, all our attention, is for that strutting turkey-cock, the war-lord whose mailed fist holds

Industrial Evolution 69

them down! That monstrous creature, with his insane egotism, his blustering and his swaggering, his curled mustachios and military poses! An epileptic degenerate, who spends his whole life in cringing terror of hereditary insanity: whose spies and police agents are invading the homes of German Socialists, searching for letters in behalf of the agents of the Czar, obtaining evidence to send men in Russia to exile and death! This ruler of his people, who the other day cashiered a near relative, an army officer who had advised soldiers to complain when they were maltreated! whose generals and admirals are swaggering about and spitting in the face of civilisation—and making maps and plans for a naval station in defiance of the Monroe Doctrine!

Forty years ago, at the time of our Civil War, when the fate of this nation hung trembling in the balance, when the Emperor of France and the aristocracy of England saw a chance to cripple republican government and to set back civilisation half a century—what was it then that prevented them? What was it but the fact that in England there existed an organised opposition, alert and watchful, trained by a generation of parliamentary conflict, and with leaders who in such a crisis could not be put down? What was it but the fact that the workers of the factory towns of Great Britain had been disciplined and taught, and could not be deceived—that they chose rather to starve than to help the cause of Slavery? And if you care to see what would have happened had not that opposition been ready, go back three- or four-score years, when the people of France struck their blow for liberty, and see the leaders of the British aristocracy crushing out protest and imprisoning objectors, and hurling the nation into a criminal and causeless war! Hear the king and the nobility, statesmen and authors, newspapers and pulpits screaming in frenzy and goading the people on, till they had desolated Europe with fifteen years of hideous slaughter, from the moral and spiritual effects of which the world has not yet recovered!

And now you stand and contemplate another such crime against civilisation. The two most enlightened peoples of the world are to come together and strip for a fight. The powers that rule in each of them made up their minds years ago, and among the officers, both in the army and in the navy of each, the coming conflict is taken for granted. Two or three years ago a German officer promised that an army corps would march from one end of this continent to the other; and an admiral in our own navy has publicly foretold the struggle. The German capitalists are in desperation for new markets, and the German people are on the edge of a revolt, with an irresponsible military despot in absolute control of them, who knows that his only chance to put off the revolution is to pick a quarrel and beat the war-drum, and summon the masses to the defence of the honour of the Fatherland. When that supreme hour comes, and when the war-lust begins to burn, upon the Social-Democratic Party of Germany will fall the task of saving civilisation; and what shall *we* have done to help them—what encouragement shall *we* have sent them? We have sent ships of grain to the cotton-operatives of Lancashire when they were starving; but what have we done for the people of Germany? What reason have we given them, with our tariffs and imperialisms, to think of us otherwise than as a nation of shopkeepers, a nation sunk in greed and commercialism, and dead to every noble impulse of men?

CHAPTER III

MARKETS AND MISERY

I GAVE in the first chapter a brief outline of my view of the process of wealth concentration. It is now time to consider the present status of affairs, and determine if we can exactly how near to completion our industrial machinery has come. Because of the vital part which the question of foreign markets has played and must play in our affairs, it is necessary that this inquiry should include a careful survey of conditions in the rest of the world.

The manufactures of the United States have grown from one hundred and ninety-eight million dollars in 1810, to five billion in 1890, and thirteen billion in 1900. Our exports to foreign countries increased from sixty-six million dollars in 1810 to eight hundred and fifty-six million in 1890, and a billion and half in 1905. Of course, if we could find unlimited markets abroad we might go on for half a century, or at least until our people grew tired of doing hard work for the rest of the world, and getting in return either bad debts, or else money to be used in building new machines

Markets and Misery 73

to do more work of the same sort. But this is not the case, as it happens; there are half a dozen nations that have been building up industrial machines of their own, and have completed them; the meaning of the Socialist movements of England and Germany and France and Belgium and Italy is simply that all these nations are now able to manufacture more than their own people are able to buy, under the old deadly combination of a monopoly price and a competitive wage. And so when we go over to Europe to look for markets, we meet people who are coming over to look for markets among us; and when in our desperation we begin to sell out at any cost, the German capitalist cries out in protest, and the German workingmen are thrown on the streets, and the German Socialists increase their vote. And when the German capitalist retaliates and sells out at cost, *our* capitalists are checked, and *our* mills are stopped— and *our* Socialist vote goes up.

Look at the figures. England was the first in the field. The output of coal of Great Britain was one hundred and fifty million dollars in 1810; it was six hundred and sixty-five million dollars in 1878; in the same period the exports of manufactures rose from two hundred and thirty million dollars to one billion dollars. All that while, of course, England ruled the sea and had things her own way. In 1820 the value of all her manufactures was about seven billion dollars—equal to that of Germany and Austria combined, or to France and the United States combined, or to all the rest of the world, excluding these four nations. But then, little by little, the others began to catch up with her: in 1880, instead of manufacturing one-fourth of the world's products, Great Britain manufactured one-fifth, and in 1894 she manufactured less than one-sixth. Between the years 1894 and 1902, British exports increased only thirteen per cent., while those of France increased sixteen per cent., those of Germany thirty-nine per cent., and those of the United States sixty-six per cent. The result was that a few years ago tens and hundreds of thousands of starving men were parading the streets of London, and all England was startled by Mr. Chamberlain's announcement that the last hope of England was a tariff which would reserve for her the trade of the colonies! Of course England could not have made money by a tariff unless her colonies had consented to lose money; and the colonies were not planning to lose money—they were counting on making some by England's tax on food. So the plan simply reduced itself to an invitation to the British workingman to pay more for his bread so that he could

Markets and Misery 75

get starvation wages for doing the manufacturing of Canada and Australia and India. Is it any wonder that the reply to the proposal should have been an independent labour vote which sent a thrill of alarm through the nation?

And meanwhile Canada and Australia and India are straining every nerve to build up manufactures of their own! "No person connected with the cotton industry can be ignorant of the progress of cotton manufactures in India," wrote the *Textile Recorder* in 1888. "Indian cotton piece-goods are coming to the front and displacing those of Manchester." The Bombay Factory Commission of the same year recorded in Parliament how this was being done. "The factory engines are at work as a rule from 5:00 A. M. to 7:00, 8:00 and 9:00 P. M. In busy times it happens that the same set of workers remain at the gins and presses night and day, with half an hour's rest in the evenings." And, like India, Canada also puts duties on British goods to protect her own growing industries!

Meanwhile, also, the rest of the world is hard at work. Let us continue viewing that same industry of cotton-spinning. The value of the manufactured-cotton product of Austria has grown from fifteen million dollars in 1834, to thirty-five million dollars in 1860, and ninety millions in 1894. The textile manufactures of Belgium trebled themselves in three years previous to 1894; those of Germany have increased twenty-fold in sixty years; those of Italy nine-fold in twenty years, while even such backward countries as Russia and Spain have doubled their textile industries, one in thirty, the other in twenty years. Most unexpected and disconcerting of all, however, is Japan, who was once looked upon as a permanent customer, but whose home industries have been growing like a magic plant. The textile manufactures of Japan doubled in value in the three years between 1896 and 1899. From six million pounds of cotton spun in 1886, Japan advanced to ninety-one million in 1893, and to one hundred and fifty-three million in 1895, in nine years increasing twenty-four fold. The value of all her textile produce was six million dollars in 1887, and it was seventy million dollars in 1895. Therefore her imports of cotton goods from Europe fell from eight million dollars in 1884 to four million in 1895.

And while this was going on in the rest of the world, in the United States the value of manufactured cotton was rising from forty-five million dollars in 1840, to two hundred and ten million dollars in 1880, to two hundred and sixty-seven million dollars in 1890, and to three hnndred and thirty-nine million in 1900! Under such

Markets and Misery 77

circumstances, is it any wonder that, at the outbreak of the Russo-Japanese war, the factories of Massachusetts and Canada were running on half-time, and dozens not running at all; that British cotton manufacturers found that prices had decreased fifteen per cent. in as many years; that the weavers of Belgium were starving, and the country was full of riots and insurrections; and that all the nations of Europe were gathering in the Far East like vultures about a carcass—knowing that the sole condition upon which any one of them could maintain its industrial and social régime for another decade, was its ability to secure the custom of some hundreds of millions of Chinamen, who are so poor that a handful of rice and a cotton shirt are all they own in the world!

I often wonder what our college presidents and other after-dinner economists make of facts such as these. They do not discuss them in their speeches. I am acquainted with only one man among all our orthodox advisers who believes in the permanence of the competitive régime, and at the same time really understands what it is and what it implies—who cares for the truth, follows his views to their conclusions, and then speaks the conclusions. When I first became acquainted with this gentleman—intellectually acquainted, that is—it affected me painfully, and even now the sight of his book gives me internal sensations akin to those of a man in an ascending elevator which comes to a sudden halt.

The book is "The New Empire," and the author is Mr. Brooks Adams. He writes coldly and dispassionately, and with the certainty of the man of science, whose conclusions may not be disputed. His style is characteristic; it is brief and to the point, and there are no apologies.

Mr. Adams is the apostle of competition. He explains that he is this, not from choice but from necessity. "Very probably keen competition is not a blessing. We cannot alter our environment. Nature has cast the United States into the vortex of the fiercest struggle ever known." His theory of life Mr. Adams condenses as follows: "For the purpose of obtaining a working hypothesis it is assumed that men are evolved from their environment like other animals, and that their intellectual, moral, and social qualities may be investigated as developments from the struggle for life. . . . Food is the first necessity, but as most regions produce food more or less abundantly, the pinch lies not so much in the existence of the food itself as with its distribution. . . . To satisfy their hunger men must not only be able to defend their own, but, in case of dearth, to rob their neighbours, where they cannot buy,

Markets and Misery 79

for the weaker must perish. . . . Life may be destroyed as effectually by peaceful competition as by war. A nation which is undersold may perish by famine as completely as if slaughtered by a conqueror. . . . For these reasons men have striven to equip themselves well for the combat, and since the end of the Stone Age no nation in the more active quarters of the globe has been able to do so without a supply of relatively cheap metal. . . . Thus the position of the mines has influenced the direction of travel. The centre of the mineral production is likely to be the seat of empire. I believe it is impossible to overestimate the effect upon civilsation of the variation of trade routes. According to the ancient tradition, the whole valley of the Syr-Daria was once so thickly settled that a nightingale could fly from branch to branch of different trees, and a cat walk from wall to wall and from housetop to housetop, from Kashgar to the Sea of Aral." But the trade route across central Asia was displaced, "and so it has come to pass that Bagdad has sunk into a mass of hovels, and the valley of Syr-Daria is a wilderness. The fate of the empire of Haroun-al-Raschid exemplifies an universal law."

"The greatest prize of modern times," in Mr. Adams's opinion, is northern China, and upon this the fate of empire rests.

His book was published in 1901, and he considered then that the chances were all with the United States. Ten years before we had been "tottering upon the brink of ruin. . . . Relief came through an exertion of energy and adaptability, perhaps without a parallel. . . . In three years America reorganised her whole social system by a process of consolidation, the result of which has been the so-called trust. But the trust is in reality the highest type of administrative efficiency, and therefore of economy, which has as yet been attained. By means of this consolidation the American people were enabled to utilise their mines to the full . . . The shock of the impact of the new power seems overwhelming. . . . In March, 1897, Pittsburg achieved supremacy in steel, and in an instant Europe felt herself poised above an abyss. . . . The Spanish Empire disintegrated, and Great Britain displayed a lassitude which has attracted the attention of the entire world. . . . Germany has also been perturbed. . . . Russia has, however, suffered most.

"The world seems agreed that the United States is likely to achieve, if indeed she has not already achieved, an economic supremacy. The vortex of the cyclone is near New York. No such activity prevails elsewhere; nowhere are undertakings so

Markets and Misery 81

gigantic, nowhere is administration so perfect; nowhere are such masses of capital centralised in single hands. And as the United States becomes an imperial market, she stretches out along the trade routes which lead from foreign countries to her heart, as every empire has stretched out from the days of Sargon to our own. The West Indies drift toward us, the Republic of Mexico hardly longer has an independent life, and the City of Mexico is an American town. With the completion of the Panama Canal all Central America will become a part of our system. We have expanded into Asia, we have attracted the fragments of the Spanish dominions, and reaching out into China, we have checked the demands of Russia and Germany, in territory, which, until yesterday, had been supposed to be beyond our sphere. We are penetrating Europe, and Great Britain especially is assuming the position of a dependency, which must rely upon us as the base from which she draws her food in peace, and without which she could not stand in war."

"Supposing the movement of the next fifty years only equal to that of the last," continues our author, . . . "the United States will outweigh any single empire, if not all empires combined. The whole world will pay her tribute. Commerce will flow to her, both from east and west, and the order which has existed from the dawn of time will be reversed."

There is only one peril about all this, in the opinion of Mr. Adams. "Society is now moving with intense velocity, and masses are gathering bulk with proportional rapidity. There is also some reason to surmise that the equilibrium is correspondingly delicate and unstable. If so apparently slight a cause as a fall of prices for a decade has been sufficient to propel the seat of empire across the Atlantic, an equally slight derangement of the administrative functions of the United States might force it across the Pacific. Prudence therefore would dictate the adoption of measures to minimise the likelihood of sudden shocks. . . . If the New Empire should develop, it must be an enormous complex mass, to be administered only by means of a cheap, elastic and simple machinery; an old and clumsy mechanism must, sooner or later, collapse, and in sinking may involve a civilisation."

By "an old and clumsy mechanism" Mr. Adams explains elsewhere that he means our American political system. Our ancestors were opposed to much consolidation, and they formed a constitution that was practically unchangeable, because they believed they had "reached certain final truths of government." "The language of the

Markets and Misery 83

Declaration of Independence, in which they proclaimed one of these truths (that all men are created equal), varies little from that of a Catholic council," says Mr. Adams. An American is apt to believe such formulas, being "dominated by tradition." But a modern thinker views them "as having no necessary relation to the conduct of affairs in the twentieth century." "If men are to be observed scientifically, the standard by which customs and institutions must be gauged cannot be abstract moral principles, but success. . . . Institutions are good when they lead to success in competition, and bad when they hinder."

The United States now forms a "gigantic and growing empire. She occupies a position of extraordinary strength. Favoured alike by geographical position, by deposits of minerals, by climate, and by the character of her population, she has little to fear either in peace or war, from rivals, provided the friction created by the movement of the masses with which she has to deal does not neutralise her energy." . . .

"The alternative presented is plain. We may cherish ideals and risk substantial benefits to realise them. Such is the emotional instinct. Or we may regard our government dispassionately, as we would any other matter of business. . . . The United States has become the heart of the economic system of the age, and she must maintain her supremacy by wit and force, or share the fate of the discarded. What that fate is the following pages tell. . . . With conservative populations *slaughter* is nature's remedy."

Never in my life shall I forget the hours in which I wrestled with these problems—the weeks and the months of perplexity and despair. It happened long before I ever heard of Mr. Adams—for of course these thoughts of his are the thoughts of the time, there is a whole literature of them, from Kipling, Roosevelt, and the Kaiser down. And to look back over the weary wastes of history—the blind, hideous nightmare of blood and tears—and then to look forward, and in all the future see nothing else! To see never any rest for agonised humanity, only kill or be killed for ages upon ages! To see this newest and noblest effort of man after freedom and peace—the American Republic—turned into an engine of slaughter and oppression! To be shown by cold, scientific formulas that my reverence for the traditions of Lincoln was merely an "emotional impulse," and that the end of it could only be that my country would share "the fate of the discarded!" I could not believe it—I cried out in the night-time for deliverance from it.

*There is a certain relentlessness about Mr. Adams, which fills the reader with rebellion, and makes him think. The average imperialist carefully avoids doing this; he veils his doctrines with moral phrases, with the decent pretence of "destiny" at the very least. But Mr. Adams dances a very war-dance upon the thing called "moral sense"—never before was it made to seem such an impertinent superfluity.

Have you, the reader, never had one smallest doubt? Does it not, for instance, seem strange to you now, when you think of it, that this mighty people cannot stay quietly at home and live their own life and mind their own affairs? How does it happen that our existence as a nation depends upon expansion? Is it that our population is growing so fast? But here is our Imperialist President lamenting that our population is not growing fast enough! And so we have to fight to find room for our children; and we have to have more children in order that we may be able to fight! We deplore race-suicide, and we give as our reason that it prevents race-murder!

Picture to yourself half a dozen men on an island. If the island be fertile they can get along without any foreign trade, can they

---

*Portions of the following argument were published as an article in the *North American Review*.

not? And then why cannot a *nation* do it? According to Mulhall, in 1894 two millions of our agricultural labourers were raising food for foreign countries. And all our imports are luxuries, save a few things such as tea and coffee and some medicines! And still our existence as a nation depends upon foreign trade—trade with Filipinos and Chinamen, with Hottentots and Esquimaux! Why?

Can you, the reader, tell me? We manufacture more than we can use, you say. Unless we can sell the balance to the Chinamen some of our factories must close down, and then some of our people would starve. But why, I ask, cannot our own starving people have the things that go abroad—some of all that food that goes abroad, for instance? Why is it that the Chinamen come first and our own people afterwards? Until we have made some things for the Chinamen, you explain, we have no money to buy anything ourselves. And so always the Chinamen first. It seems such a strange, upside-down arrangement—does it not seem so to you? For, look you, the people of England are in the same fix, and the people of Germany are in the same fix—the people of all the competing nations are in the same fix! They actually have to go to war to kill each other, in order to get a chance to sell something

Markets and Misery

to the Chinamen, so that they can get money to buy some things for themselves! They were actually doing that in Manchuria for eighteen months! More amazing yet, they had to go and murder some of the Chinamen, in order to compel the rest to buy something, so that they could get money to buy something for themselves!

How long can it be possible for a human being, with a spark of either conscience or brains in him, to gaze at such a state of affairs and not *know* that there is something wrong about it? And how long could he gaze before the truth of it would flash over him—that the reason for it is that some private party owns all the machinery and materials of production, and will not give the people anything, until they have first made something that can be sold! That all the world lies at the mercy of those who own the materials and machinery, and who leave men to starve when they cannot make profits! And that this is why we Americans cannot stay at home and be happy, but are forced to go trading with Filipinos and Chinamen, Hottentots and Esquimaux, and competing for "empire" with our brothers in England and Germany and Japan!

If the reader be an average American, these thoughts will be new to him. He has been brought up on a diet of misunderstood Malthusianism. He is told that life has always been a struggle for existence and always will be; that there is not food enough to go round, and that therefore, every now and then, the surplus population has to be cut down by famine an war. It is to be pointed out concerning the doctrine that, while he swears allegiance to it, he doesn't like to think about it, and when it comes to the practical test he shows that he does not really believe it. Whenever famine comes, he subscribes to a grain-fund, and does his best to defeat nature; when war comes, he gets up a Red Cross Society for the same purpose. And yet he still continues to swear by this wiping out of the nations, and any discussion about abolishing poverty he waves aside as Utopian.

The writer may fail in his purpose with this paper. but he will not have written in vain if he can lead a few men to see the pitiful folly of that half-baked theory which ranks men with the wild beasts of the jungle, and ignores the existence of both science and morality. He can do that, assuredly, with any one whom he can induce to read one little book—Prince Kropotkin's "Fields, Factories and Workshops."

The book was published nine years ago, but apparently it has not yet had time to affect the cogitations of the orthodox economists. You still read, as you have been used to reading since the days of Adam

Markets and Misery

Smith, that the possibilities of the soil are strictly limited, and that population always stays just within the starvation limit. Nearly all the fertile land in this country, for instance, is now in use, and so we shall soon reach the limit here. The forty million people of Great Britain have long since passed it, and they would starve to death were it not for our surplus. And there are portions of the world where population is even more dense, as in Belgium. All this you have known from your school-days, and you think you know it perfectly, and beyond dispute; and so how astonished you will be to be told that it is simply one of the most stupid and stupefying delusions that ever were believed and propagated among men; that the limits of the productive possibilities of the soil have not only not been attained, but are, so far as science can now see, absolutely unattainable; that not only could England support with ease her own population on her own soil, and not only could Belgium do it, but any most crowded portion of the world could do it, and do it once again, and yet once again, and do it with two or three hours of work a day by a small portion of its population! That England could now support, not merely her thirty-three million inhabitants, but seventy-five and perhaps a hundred million! And that the United States could now support a billion and a quarter of people, or just about the entire population of this planet! And that this could be done year after year, and entirely without any possibility of the exhaustion of the soil! And all this not any theory of a closet speculator or a Utopian dreamer, but by methods that are used year after year by thousands and tens of thousands of men who are making money by it in all portions of the world—in the market-gardens of Paris and London, of Belgium, Holland and the island of Jersey, the truck-farms of Florida and Minnesota, and of Norfolk, Virginia!

Prince Kropotkin writes:

"While science devotes its chief attention to industrial pursuits, a limited number of lovers of nature and a legion of workers, whose very names will remain unknown to posterity, have created of late a quite new agriculture, as superior to modern farming as modern farming is superior to the old three-fields system of our ancestors. They smile when we boast about the rotation system having permitted us to take from the field one crop every year, or four crops every three years, because their ambition is to have six and nine crops from the very same plot of land every twelve months. They do not understand our talk about good and bad soils, because they make the

Markets and Misery 91

soil themselves, and make it in such quantities as to be compelled yearly to sell some of it; otherwise, it would raise up the levels of their gardens by half an inch every year. They aim at cropping, not five or six tons of grass to the acre, as we do, but from fifty to one hundred tons of various vegetables on the same space; not twenty-five dollars' worth of hay, but five hundred dollars' worth of vegetables, of the plainest description, cabbages and carrots. That is where agriculture is going now."

The writer tells about all these things in detail. Here is the *culture maraîchere* of Paris—a M. Ponce, with a tiny orchard of two and seven-tenths acres, for which he pays five hundred dollars rent a year, and from which he takes produce that could not be named short of several pages of figures: twenty thousand pounds of carrots, twenty thousand of onions and radishes, six thousand heads of cabbage, three thousand of cauliflower, five thousand baskets of tomatoes, five thousand dozen choice fruit, one hundred and fifty-four thousand heads of "salad"—in all, two hundred and fifty thousand pounds of vegetables. Says the author:

"The Paris gardener not only defies the soil—he would grow the same crops on an asphalt pavement—he defies climate. His walls, which are built to reflect light and to protect the wall-trees from the northern winds, his wall-tree shades and glass protectors, his *pépinières*, have made a rich Southern garden out of the suburbs of Paris."

The consequence of this is that the population of the districts of that city, three millions and a half of people, could, if it were necessary, be maintained in their own territory, provided with food both animal and vegetable, from a piece of ground less than sixty miles on a side! And at the same time, by the same methods, they are raising thirty tons of potatoes on an acre in Minnesota, and three hundred and fifty bushels of corn in Iowa, and six hundred bushels of onions in Florida. And with machinery, on the prairie wheat-farms, they raise crops at a cost which makes twelve hours and a half of work *of all kinds* enough to supply a man with the flour part of his food for a year! And then, as if to cap the climax, comes Mr. Horace Fletcher with his discovery that all the ailments of civilised man, (including old age and death) are due to overeating; and Professor Chittenden with his practical demonstration that the quantity of food needed by man is about four-tenths of what all physiologists have previously taught! *And while all this has been

---

*Horace Fletcher: "The A-B-Z of Our Own Nutrition." R. L. Chittenden: "Physiological Economy in Nutrition."

Courtesy of Wilshire's Magazine

Courtesy of Wilshire's Magazine

REAPING BY HAND AND BY MACHINERY

Markets and Misery 93

going on for a decade, while encyclopedias have been written about it, our political economists continue to discuss wages and labour, rent and interest, exchange and consumption, from the standpoint of the dreary, century-old formula that there must always be an insufficient supply of food in the world! Such is the state of affairs with agriculture: and now how is it with everything else? In the Thirteenth Annual Report of the Commissioner of Labour (1898), Carroll D. Wright has figured the relative costs of doing various pieces of work by hand and by modern machinery. Here are a few of the cases he gives:

"*Making of* 10 *plows:* By hand, 2 workmen, performing 11 distinct operations, working a total of 1,180 hours, and paid $54.46. By machine, 52 workmen, 97 operations, 37½ hours, $7.90.

"*Making of* 500 *lbs. of butter:* By hand, 3 men, 7 operations, 125 hours, $10.66. By machine, 7 men, 8 operations, 12½ hours, $1.78.

"*Making of* 500 *yds. twilled cottonade:* By hand, 3 men, 19 operations 7,534 hours, $135.61. By machine, 252 men, 43 operations, 84 hours, $6.81.

"*Making of* 100 *pairs of cheap boots:* By hand, 2 workmen, 83 operations, 1,436 hours, $408.50. By machine, 113 workmen, 122 operations, 154 hours, $35.40."

Thus we see human labour has been cut to the extent of from eighty to ninety-five per cent. From other sources I have gathered a few facts about the latest machinery. In Pennsylvania, some sheep were shorn and the wool turned into clothing in six hours, four minutes. A steer was killed, its hide tanned, turned into leather and made into shoes in twenty-four hours. The ten million bottles used by the Standard Oil Company every year are now blown by machinery. An electric riveting-machine puts rivets in steel-frame buildings at the rate of two per minute. Two hundred and sixty needles per minute, ten million match-sticks per day, five hundred garments cut per day—each by a machine tended by one little boy. The newest weaving-looms run through the dinner hour and an hour and a half after the factory closes, making cloth with no one to tend them at all. The new basket-machine invented by Mergenthaler, the inventor of the linotype, is now in operation everywhere, "making fruit-baskets, berry-baskets and grape-baskets of a strength and quality never approached by hand labour. Fancy a single machine that will turn out completed berry-baskets at the rate of twelve thousand per day of nine hours' work! This is at the rate of one thousand three hundred per hour, or over twenty baskets a minute! One girl, operating

Markets and Misery   95

this machine, does the work of twelve skilled hand operators!"

Since all these wonders are the commonplace facts of modern industry, it is not surprising that here and there men should begin to think about them; here is the naïve question recently asked by the editor of a Montreal newspaper which I happened on:

"With the best of machinery at the present day, one man can produce woollens for three hundred people. One man can produce boots and shoes for one thousand people. One man can produce bread for two hundred people. Yet thousands cannot get woollens, boots and shoes, or bread. *There must be some reason for this state of affairs.*"

There is a reason, a perfectly plain and simple reason, which all over the world the working-people, whom it concerns, are coming to understand. The reason is that all the woollen manufactories, the boot and shoe and bread manufactories, and all the sources of the raw materials of these, and all the means of handling and distributing them when they are manufactured, belong to a few private individuals instead of to the community as a whole. And so, instead of the cotton-spinner, the shoe-operative and the bread-maker having free access to them, to work each as long as he pleases, produce as much as he cares to, and exchange his products for as much of the products of other workers as he needs, each one of these workers can only get at the machines by the consent of another man, and then does not get what he produces, but only a small fraction of it, and does not get that except when the owner of the balance can find some one with money enough to buy that balance at a profit to him!

Prof. Hertzka, the Austrian economist, in his "Laws of Social Evolution," has elaborately investigated the one real question of political economy to-day, the actual labour and time necessary for the creation, under modern conditions, of the necessaries of life for a people. Here are the results for the Austrian people, of twenty-two million:

"It takes 26,250,000 acres of agricultural land, and 7,500,000 of pasturage, for all agricultural products. Then I allowed a house to be built for every family, consisting of five rooms. I found that all industries, agriculture, architecture, building, flour, sugar, coal, iron, machine-building, clothing, and chemical production, need 615,000 labourers employed 11 hours per day, 300 days a year, to satisfy every imaginable want for 22,000,000 inhabitants.

"These 615,000 labourers are only 12.3 per cent. of the population able to do work, excluding women and all persons under 16 or over 50 years of age; all these latter to be considered as not able.

Markets and Misery 97

"Should the 5,000,000 able men be engaged in work, instead of 615,000, they need only to work 36.9 days every year to produce everything needed for the support of the population of Austria. But should the 5,000,000 work all the year, say 300 days—which they would probably have to do to keep the supply fresh in every department—each one would only work 1 hour and 22½ minutes per day.

"But to engage to produce all the *luxuries*, in addition, would take, in round figures, 1,000,000 workers, classed and assorted as above, or only 20 per cent. of all those able, excluding every woman, or every person under 16 or over 50, as before. The 5,000,000 able, strong male members could produce everything imaginable for the whole nation of 22,000,000 in 2 hours and 12 minutes per day, working 300 days a year."

But then you say: If this be true, if two hours' work will produce everything, how can everybody go on working twelve hours forever? They can't; and that is just why I am writing this book. They can do it only until they have filled the needs, first of themselves, then of all the Filipinos and Chinamen, Hottentots and Esquimaux who have money to buy anything—and then until they have filled all the factories, warehouses and stores of the country to overflowing. Then they cannot do one single

thing more; then they are out of work
They can go on so long as their masters can
find a market in which to sell their product at
a profit; then they have to stop. And then
suddenly (*instantly*, God help them!) they
have to take their choice between two alternatives—between an Industrial Republic,
and a political empire. Either they will
hear Prince Kropotkin, or they will hear
Mr. Brooks Adams. Either they will take
the instruments and means of production
and produce for use and not for profit; or
else they will forge themselves into an engine
of war to be wielded by a military despot.
In that case, they will fling themselves
upon China and Japan, and seize northern
China, "the greatest prize of modern times."
They will enter upon a career of empire,
and by the wholesale slaughter of war they
will keep down population, while at the
same time by the wholesale destruction of
war they keep down the surplus of products.
So there will be more work for the workers
for a time, and more profits for the masters
for a time; until what wealth there is in
northern China has also been concentrated
and possessed, when once more there will
begin distress. By that time, however, we
shall have an hereditary aristocracy strongly
intrenched, and a proletariat degraded beyond recall; so that our riots will end in
mere slaughter and waste, and we shall

Markets and Misery 99

never again see freedom. We shall run then the whole course of the Roman Empire—of frenzied profligacy among the wealthy, and beastly ferocity among the populace: until at last we fall into imbecility, and are overwhelmed by some new, clean race which the strong heart of nature has poured out.

Empires have risen and have fallen; but it has not been, as Mr. Adams asserts, because of "variations of trade-routes," but solely because of wealth-concentration, with its ensuing corruption, ignorance and brutality among the populace, and avarice and luxury among the rich. Let the reader take Froude's "Cæsar," and read, in the first chapter, his picture of the last days of the Roman Republic:

"An age in so many ways the counterpart of our own, the blossoming period of the old civilisation, when the intellect was trained to the highest point that it could reach, and on the great subjects of human interest, on morals and politics, on poetry and art, even on religion itself and the speculative problems of life, men thought as we think, doubted where we doubt, argued as we argue, aspired and struggled after the same objects. It was an age of material progress and material civilisation; an age of civil liberty and intellectual culture; an age of pamphlets and epigrams, of salons and of dinner-parties, or senatorial majorities and electoral corruption, The highest offices of state were open in theory to the meanest citizen; they were confined, in fact, to those who had the longest purses, or the most ready use of the tongue on popular platforms. Distinctions of birth had been exchanged for distinctions of wealth. The struggles between plebeians and patricians for equality of privilege were over, and a new division had been formed between the party of property and a party that desired a change in the structure of society. The free cultivators were disappearing from the soil. Italy was being absorbed into vast estates, held by a few favoured families and cultivated by slaves, while the old agricultural population was driven off the land, and was crowded into towns. The rich were extravagant, for life had ceased to have practical interest, except for its material pleasures; the occupation of the higher classes was to obtain money without labour, and to spend it in idle enjoyment. Patriotism survived on the lips, but patriotism meant the ascendancy of the party which would maintain the existing order of things, or would overthrow it for a more equal distribution of the good things which alone were valued. Religion, once the foundation of the laws and rule of personal conduct, had subsided into opinion. The educated in

Markets and Misery 101

their hearts disbelieved it. Temples were still built with increasing splendour; the established forms were scrupulously observed. Public men spoke conventionally of Providence, that they might throw on their opponents the odium of impiety; but of genuine belief that life had any serious meaning there was none remaining beyond the circle of the silent, patient, ignorant multitude."

Is not this a parallel to make one pause and think? And if our American republic is to escape the fate of Rome, to what cause will it be due? The Roman failure was due to the fact that "the men and women by whom the hard work of the world was done were chiefly slaves"; those who held the franchise, the free Roman citizens, were a comparatively small class, and the patricans bought them with "bread and circuses," and so held the reins of power. In our present time, however, those who do the work and those who have the ballot are the same class; and also they have the public school and the press, and the whole of modern science at their backs. More important yet—the all-dominating fact—is the machine. The Roman chattel-slave worked with his hands, while the modern wage-slave works with tools of gigantic speed and power; which means that our modern economic process, while infinitely more cruel and destructive, makes up for these qualities by the certainty and swiftness with which it rushes to its end. So it is that a Revolution which in Rome took centuries to culminate and fail, will require only decades in America to accomplish its inevitable triumph.

CHAPTER IV

SOCIAL DECAY

IF MY analysis of the industrial process be correct, there will be two developments observable in our society: the first a material change, a kind of economic apoplexy, the concentration of wealth in one portion of society, accompanied by an intensification of competition, a falling in the rate of interest, and a steady rise in the cost of living; and second, a spiritual change coincident with the material one, a protest against the rising frenzy of greed, and against the constantly increasing economic pressure.

It is important that these two processes should be clearly perceived, and their relationship correctly understood; for there is no aspect of the whole problem about which there is more bad thinking done. The two are cause and effect, and they explain and prove each other; and yet almost invariably you will hear them cited as contradicting each other. If, for instance, one speaks of the ever-rising tide of misery and suffering in our society, he will be met with the response that "the world is getting better all the time." And when he asks for some proof of the statement, the reply will be that a great national awakening is going on, that we are developing new ideals and a new public spirit!

Similarly I have, time and again, when advocating this or that concrete remedy, been met with the statement that the cure for the evils of the time is publicity—that the people must be educated—that we must appeal to men's moral sense, etc. It is useless to argue with a person who cannot perceive that all these things are simply means to an end, and not the end. You cannot educate people just to be educated; when you appeal to them, you have to appeal to them to *do* something.

One cannot insist too strongly upon the futility of sentiment in connection with this process. We are dealing with facts, with grim and brutal and merciless reality. And it will not avail you to try to smooth it over—it will not do any good to turn your head and refuse to face it. Here is the monster machine of competition, grinding remorselessly on; the wealth of the world is rushing with cyclonic speed into one portion of the social body, and in the other portion whole classes of men and women and children are being swept out of existence, are being wiped off the economic slate. Exactly as capital piles up—at compounded and

Social Decay

re-compounded interest—so also piles up the mass of human misery of every conceivable sort—luxury, debauchery and cynicism at the top, prostitution, suicide, insanity, and crime at the bottom. Political corruption spreads further and eats deeper, business practice becomes more impersonal and more ruthless; and all progress awaits the swing of the pendulum, the time when the cumulative pressure of all this mass of misery shall have driven the people to frenzy, and forced them to overturn the system of class exploitation and greed.

I purpose to cite in detail the symptoms of disease and decay in our body politic; before I begin, I wish to put my interpretation of them into one sentence, which a man can carry away with him. I say that the evils of our time are due without exception to one single cause—*that our people are being driven, with constantly increasing rigour, to the ultimately hopeless task of paying interest upon a mass of capital which is increasing at compound interest.*

Consider in the first place the broader aspect of the situation—the dollar-madness of the time which is the staple theme of the moralist. I have a friend who is in control of a great business concern, and who will read this little book with intense disapproval; and yet so fearfully has this man been driven by the lash of competition that when I saw him last he could scarcely digest a bit of dry bread, and his hand trembled so that he could hardly lift a glass of water to his lips. He talked of his business in his sleep, and he could not go for a walk and forget it for five minutes. And why? Was it money? He has so much that his family could not spend it if they lived a hundred years; but it was his business, it was his life. He was caught in the mill and he could not get out. His is one of those few industries which have not yet formed a trust, and he is in the last gasp of the competitive struggle—he has to plot and plan day and night to get new orders, and to cut down expenses, and to keep up the dividends upon which his *reputation* rests.

And as it is with him, so it is with the rest of us. We have to play the game; we have to cut our neighbour's throat, knowing that otherwise our neighbour will cut ours. And year after year the pressure of the whole thing grows more tense. Suicide in the United States has increased from twelve per one hundred thousand of population in the year 1890, to sixteen in the year 1896, and seventeen in the year 1902; in Germany it rose from twenty to nearly twenty-two in the three years between 1900 and 1903; in England it rose from thirty in 1894, to thirty-fivein 1904. According to the *Civiltà*

Social Decay

Cattolica the frequency of this crime in Europe has increased four hundred per cent. while population has increased only sixty per cent.; and there have been over one million suicides recorded in the last twenty-five years. There were ninety-two thousand insane persons in the United States in 1880, one hundred and six thousand in 1890, and one hundred and forty-five thousand in 1896. Per one thousand of population, there were twenty-nine prisoners in 1850, sixty-one in 1860, eighty-five in 1870, one hundred and seventeen in 1880, and one hundred and thirty-two in 1890. In 1876 the population of this country consumed eight and sixty-one one-hundredths gallons of liquor per capita; in 1890 they consumed fifteen and fifty-three one-hundredths, and in 1902 they consumed nineteen and forty-eight one-hundredths. The actual consumption at the last date was a billion and a half of gallons. These figures take but a few lines to state; and yet no human imagination can form any conception of the frightful mass of human anguish which they imply. They constitute in themselves a proof of the thesis here advanced, that there is at work in our society some great and fundamental evil force.*

---

*"An experienced magistrate, Recorder John W. Goff of New York, told me not long since that in his judgment the course of crime in this country is not only towards more frequency and gravity, but that it is changing its old hot impulsiveness, openness and directness for cold calculation, secretiveness and deliberate intention to strike without being discovered This progress and difference he attributes mediately and immediately to extending and deepening poverty." Henry George. "The Menace of Privilege."

Whenever the administrators of our "constantly increasing mass of capital" find they are no longer making profits, they either reduce wages, or raise the price of their product. One or the other they must do, because without profits the machine cannot run. When good times come they sometimes raise the wages again—because of the unions; but they never lower the price of the product—the poor consumer is a non-union man. Two years ago Mr. Rockefeller put up the price of oil one cent, and the Beef Trust has done the same about once a year. And of course a general increase in prices is exactly the same as a general cut in wages—in either case the consumer has to work a little harder to make ends meet, and if he cannot work harder, he dies. The coal-miners rejoiced in the award of the Commission, untroubled by the extra fifty cents the coal companies put on the product; but when the miner comes to add up his account with the butcher and the oil man, he finds he is just where he was before. He does not know why, you understand—it is merely that he finds himself compelled to do without something he used to consider a necessity. Dun's Review, figuring the cost of living in the United States upon a basis of 100, puts it at 72.455 in 1897, and 102.208 in 1904—an increase of forty-one per cent. Bradstreet, reckon-

Social Decay

ing in another way, shows an increase from 6.51 in 1897, to 9.05 in 1904, or thirty-nine per cent. According to the annual report of the Commissary General, United States Army, the cost of feeding the soldiers of the army has increased from eighteen cents in 1898 to thirty-four and six-tenths cents in 1903. Statisticians have figured that the average employee earns ninety dollars a year more than he did twenty years ago, while it costs him to live on the same scale, one hundred and thirty dollars a year more. According to the last United States census the average compensation per wage earner was only three hundred and forty dollars, while the value of the manufactured product was two thousand four hundred and fifty dollars per wage earner. Perhaps no clearer statement of the intensification of exploitation can be found than in the fact that whereas the average profit on the products of all industries was three hundred and seventy-five dollars per wage earner in 1880, in 1900 it had increased to six hundred and twenty-six dollars.

Another consequence of the increasing strain is "race suicide"; which is simply a popular term for that "elimination of the middle class" which Karl Marx predicted half a century ago. The homilies of President Roosevelt may have caused a few more superfluous bourgeois babies to be born;

but I rather fancy that in general it has been a case of "everybody's business and nobody's business" — that the average middle-class American has no idea of lowering his standard of living for the purpose of affecting the census returns. As a result of a confidential census of "race suicide," taken in England and reported in the *Popular Science Monthly*, Mr. Sidney Webb found that the offspring had been voluntarily limited in two hundred and twenty-four cases out of a total of two hundred and fifty-two marriages; and out of the one hundred and twenty-eight cases in which the causes of limitation were given, economic causes were specified in seventy-three. Similar results would certainly follow an inquiry in this country; in fact Americans of refinement have come to have an instinctive feeling of repugnance to a large family; to have six or seven children is vulgar and "common," and suggestive of foreigners. The reason is simply that conditions now prevail which make large families impossible, except to Poles and Hungarians and Italians and French-Canadians, people who are too ignorant to limit their offspring, and whose standards of life are close to animals—their children earning their own livings in sweatshops, mines and factories, as soon as they are able to walk.

And yet, low as our lowest classes have

been ground, they are not low enough. Thousands of agents of steamship companies are gathering the outcasts from the sewers of Europe and shipping them here. The rate of immigration into this country was three hundred and eleven thousand in 1899, four hundred and eighty-seven thousand in 1901, six hundred and forty-eight thousand in 1902, eight hundred and fifty-seven thousand in 1903, and over a million in 1905—more than one-half of the last shipments being from Hungary, Russia, and southern Italy. All this, you must understand, is managed by the "System" which rules in our centres of industry. "In that unhappy anthracite country," writes Mr. John Graham Brooks, a person of authority, "the employers will tell you openly, and with conscious bravado, that they must get cheaper and cheaper labour to keep wages down, else they could make no money." And it was recently estimated by George W. Morgan, State Superintendent of Elections in New York, that in one past year over six hundred thousand dollars profit was made by selling false naturalisation papers. The Federal authorities who had been investigating the frauds believed that over one hundred thousand sets of such papers had been sold, and that thirty thousand of these had been issued in New York City. Fully thirty per cent. of the Italian citizens in the southern district of New York were estimated to hold false papers.

Cheaper and cheaper labour! Women's labour and children's labour! Over one million of women are at present working in factories alone in this country; and one million and three-quarters of children between ten and fifteen years of age are engaged in gainful occupations. In the cotton factories of the South, while the number of men employed increased seventy-nine per cent. in the past ten years, the number of women increased one hundred and fifty-eight per cent. and the number of children under sixteen increased two hundred and seventy per cent. The number employed in Alabama alone was estimated by the Committee on Child Labour to be fifty thousand, with thirty-four per cent. of them under twelve years, and ten per cent. under *ten* years. These children work twelve hours a day, and the oldest get fifty cents and the youngest get nine cents. Here are the descriptions of observers:

"A little boy of six years has been working 12 hours a day, from 6:20 A. M. to 6:20 P. M. (40 minutes off at noon), for 15 cents per day.

"Three boys aged respectively 9, 8, and 7 years. The boy aged 9 has been working two years, the boy aged 8 has been working three years; the boy aged 7 years has been

Social Decay

working two years. These little fellows work 13 hours a day, from 5:20 A. M. to 6:30 P. M., with twenty minutes for dinner. In 'rush' periods their mill works until 9:30 and 10 P. M. They were refused a holiday for Thanksgiving and they obtained Christmas Day only by working till 7 P. M. in order to make up the time."

Mrs. Irene Ashby-Macfadden says: "I have talked with a little boy of seven years, in Alabama, who worked for forty nights; and another child not nine years old, who at six years old had been on the night shift eleven months."

Miss Jane Addams, of Chicago, says: "In South Carolina, in a large new mill, I found a child of five working at night. In Columbia, S. C., in a mill controlled by Northern capital, I stood at ten-thirty at night and saw many children who did not know their own ages, working from 6 P. M. to 6. A. M."

Here is a description of their surroundings:

"An atmosphere redolent of oil, thick with lint, the deafening, incessant whir of machinery, in summer stifling heat, always the insensate machinery claiming the strained attention of young eyes and tiny fingers, broken threads clamorously crying for adjustment, all requiring not hard work, but incessant vigilance, springing feet and nimble fingers. Young eyes watching anxiously for a fault in these intricately constructed machines, paying with crushed or broken members for an error in judgment, for the crime of carelessness, how must the responsibility—lightly smiled at by adults—weigh upon the barely developed intelligence of a young child? And after long hours, lagging footsteps, throbbing heads, wandering attention—what sort of stone is this, O Brothers, to be placed in the children's hands who cry for bread?"

Several years ago I saw in the *Independent* an advertisement setting forth the advantages of the State of Alabama as an investing-place for capital. I wish I had cut it out. The point of it was that there were no "labour-troubles" in Alabama; the boycott being prohibited there, and labour unions being sued for damages and smashed. The advertisement might have added that there is no factory-legislation to amount to anything, and that the percentage of native white illiteracy is fourteen and e ght-tenths. There *is* factory-legislation in Massachusetts, and it is enforced, and the percentage of native white illiteracy is only eight-tenths of one per cent., or one-eighteenth of the proportion of Alabama. So in the last overproduction crisis the mills of Alabama were running, while those of Massachusetts were shut down; and the special correspondence of the New

CHILD LABOR IN GLASS FACTORIES AND COAL MINES

Social Decay

York *Evening Post* contained the following pregnant item:

"ATLANTA, Ga., June 12—'The sceptre of commercial supremacy is falling from the palsied hand of New England industry; apparently it is to be taken up by the South. Grasp it firmly. The whole country, torn by labour disputes, looks to the South to make the final stand against legislative encroachments on the liberty of the individual workman and the individual employer.'

"So Daniel Davenport of Bridgeport, Conn., spoke to the members of the Georgia Industrial Association, at their annual convention at Warm Springs, Ga., last week. This association was one of the earliest to recognise the depressing effect of restrictive labour legislation upon the cotton manufacturing of New England; its members fear that similar legislation in the South would be followed by even more disastrous consequences, and what has injuriously affected the more hardy and older establishments of the North, would, they believe, stunt the growth of the infant industries of the South, if it did not actually crush them."

I made an effort in "The Jungle" to show what is happening to the wage-earner in our modern highly concentrated industries, under the régime of a monopoly price and a competitive wage. I spent seven weeks in Packingtown studying conditions there, and I verified every smallest detail, so that as a picture of social conditions the book is as exact as a government report. But the reader does not have to take my word for it, there are any number of studies by independent investigators. Let him go to a library and consult the American Journal of Sociology for March, 1901, and read the reports of a graduate of the University of Chicago, who investigated the conditions in the garment-trade in that city. Here were girls working ten hours a day for forty cents a week. The average of all the "dressmakers" was but ninety cents a week, and they were able to find employment on the average only forty-two weeks in the year. The "pants-finishers" received a dollar and thirty-one cents, and they were employed only twenty-seven weeks in the year. The general average in the entire trade was less than two dollars and a half a week, and the average number of weeks of work was only thirty-one, *making an average yearly wage for a whole industry of seventy-six dollars and seventy-four cents per year.* Or let the reader get Mr. Jacob A. Riis's pictures of conditions in the slums of New York. In his book, "How the Other Half Lives," Mr. Riis states that in the block bounded by Stanton, Houston, Attorney and Ridge streets, the size of which is two hundred by three hundred feet, are two thousand two

Social Decay

hundred and forty-four human beings. In the block bounded by Sixty-first and Sixty-second streets, Amsterdam and West End avenues, are over four thousand. Jack London, in his "War of The Classes," quotes the Rev. Dr. Behrends, speaking of the block bounded by Hester, Canal, Eldridge and Forsyth Streets: "In a room twelve feet by eight, and five and a half feet high, it was found that nine persons slept and prepared their food. In another room, located in a dark cellar, without screens or partitions, were together two men with their wives and a girl of fourteen, two single men and a boy of seventeen, two women and four boys, nine, ten, eleven and fifteen years old—fourteen persons in all!" Apropos of this it may be well to add that an investigation conducted in Berlin established the fact that with families living in one room the death rate was one hundred and sixty-three per thousand, while with families living in three or four rooms it was twenty. What it was with three or four families living in one room does not appear. According to a recent report of the New York Tenement House Commission there were four hundred thousand "dark rooms"—rooms without any outside opening whatever. Mr. Riis has been so successful in battling with such conditions that he has been called by President Roosevelt "the most useful

American." Neither the President nor Mr. Riis understand economics, and so probably they are both perplexed at the result of his ten years of effort—which is that rents on the East Side have gone up about fifty per cent. in the last two years, and there have been riots and evictions—and a Socialist all but elected to Congress!

But Mr. Riis is a business man, and he can figure the social cost of these evil conditions. Of the New York tenements he writes:

"They are the hot beds of epidemics that carry death to the rich and poor alike; the nurseries of pauperism and crime that fill our jails and police courts; that throw off a scum of forty thousand human wrecks to the island asylums and workhouses year by year; that turned out in the last eight years a round half million beggars to prey upon our charities; that maintain a standing army of ten thousand tramps with all that that implies; because, above all, they taint the family life with deadly moral contagion."

In his newly published discussion of social problems called "In the Fire of the Heart," Mr. Ralph Waldo Trine writes of the country's situation as follows:

"And over ten millions of our people are in a state of chronic poverty at this very hour—almost one out of every seven, or,

Social Decay

to make full allowance, one out of every eight of all our people are in the condition where they' have not sufficient food, and clothing, and shelter to keep them in a state of physical and mental efficiency. And the sad part of it is that large additional numbers—numbers most appalling for such a country as this, are each year, and through no fault of their own, dropping into this same condition.

"And a still sadder feature of it is, that each year increasingly large numbers of this vast army of people, our fellow-beings, are, unwillingly on their part and in the face of almost superhuman efforts to keep out of it till the last moment, dropping into the pauper class—those who are compelled to seek or to receive aid from a public, or from private charity, in order to exist at all, already in numbers about four million, while increasing numbers of this class, the pauper, sink each year, and so naturally, into the vicious, the criminal, the inebriate class. In other words, we have gradually allowed to be built around us a social and economic system which yearly drives vast numbers of hitherto fairly well-to-do, strong, honest, earnest, willing and admirable men with their families into the condition of poverty, and under its weary, endeavour-strangling influences many of these in time, hoping against hope, struggling to the last moment in their semi-incapacitated and pathetic manner to keep out of it, are forced to seek or to accept public or private charity, and thus sink into the pauper class.

"It is a well-authenticated fact that strong men, now weakened by poverty, will avoid it to the last before they will take this step. Many after first parting with everything they have, break down and cry like babes when the final moment comes, and they can avoid it no longer. Numbers at this time take their own lives rather than pass through the ordeal, and still larger numbers desert their families for whom they have struggled so valiantly—it is almost invariably the woman who makes her way to the charity agencies. The public and private charities cost the country during the past year as nearly as can be *conservatively* arrived at, over two hundred million dollars.

"Moreover, a strange law seems to work with an accuracy that seems almost marvellous. It is this. Notwithstanding the brave and almost superhuman struggles that are gone through with, on the part of these, before they can take themselves to the public or private charity for aid, when the step is once taken, they gradually sink into the condition where all initiative and all sense of self-reliance seems to be stifled or lost, and it is only in a rare case now and then

Social Decay

that they ever cease to be dependent, but remain content with the alms that are doled out to them—practically never do they rise out of that condition again. Talk with practically any charity agent or worker, one with a sufficiently extended experience, and you will find that there is scarcely more than one type of testimony concerning this. And as this condition gradually becomes chronic, and endeavour and initiative and self-respect are lost, a certain proportion then sink into the condition of the criminal, the diseased, the chronically drunk, the inebriate, from which reclamation is still more difficult."

The fullest and most authoritative treatise upon conditions in America is of course Mr. Robert Hunter's "Poverty." Mr. Hunter is a settlement-worker, and he has gathered his material in the midst of the conditions of which he writes. He quotes, for instance, the following definite facts, which are obtained from official sources:

"1903: twenty per cent. of the people of Boston in distress.

"1897: nineteen per cent. of the people of New York state in distress.

"1899: eighteen per cent. of the people of New York state in distress.

"1903: fourteen per cent. of the families of Manhattan evicted.

"Every year ten per cent. (about) of those

who die in Manhattan have pauper burials."

"On the basis of these figures," Mr. Hunter continues, "it would seem fair to estimate that certainly not less than fourteen per cent. of the people, in prosperous times (1903), and probably not less than twenty per cent. in bad times (1897), are in distress. The estimate is a conservative one, for despite all the imperfections which may be found in the data, and there are many, any allowance for the persons who are given aid by sources not reporting to the State Board, or for those persons not aided by the authorities of Boston, or for those persons who, although in great distress, are not evicted, must counterbalance the duplications or errors which may exist in the figures either of distress or evictions.

"These figures, furthermore, represent only the distress which manifests itself. There is no question but that only a part of of those in poverty, in any community, apply for charity. I think anyone living in a Settlement will support me in saying that many families who are obviously poor— that is, underfed, underclothed, or badly housed—never ask for aid or suffer the social disgrace of eviction. Of course, no one could estimate the proportion of those who are evicted or of those who ask assistance to the total number in poverty; for whatever opinion one may have formed is based, not

Social Decay 123

on actual knowledge, gained by inquiry, but on impressions, gained through friendly intercourse, My own opinion is that probably not over half of those in poverty ever apply for charity, and certainly not more than that proportion are evicted from their homes. However, I should not wish an opinion of this sort to be used in estimating, from the figures of distress, etc., the number of those in poverty. And yet from the facts of distress, as given, and from opinions formed, both as a charity agent and as a Settlement worker, I should not be at all surprised if the number of those in poverty in New York, as well as in other large cities and industrial centres, rarely fell below twenty-five per cent. of all the people."

Such are the conditions in America to-day; what they would be in the future, if present tendencies went on unchecked, the reader may learn by going to Europe, where industrial evolution has been slower in coming to a head, and where the people have been held down by religious superstition and military despotism. Let him take Mr. Richard Whiteing's "No. 5 John Street"; or, if he has a particularly strong stomach, let him try Jack London's "People of the Abyss," or Charles Edward Russell's terrifying story of the poverty of India, in his "Soldiers of the Common Good." Here is a scene in a London park, selected, by way of example, from the first-named book:

"We went up the narrow, gravelled walk. On the benches on either side was arrayed a mass of miserable and diseased humanity, the sight of which would have impelled Doré to more diabolical flights of fancy than he ever succeeded in achieving. It was a welter of filth and rags, of all manner of loathesome skin-diseases, open sores, bruises, grossness, indecency, leering monstrosities and bestial faces. A chill, raw wind was blowing, and these creatures huddled there in their rags, sleeping for the most part, or trying to sleep. Here were a dozen women, ranging in age from twenty years to seventy. Next a babe, possibly nine months old, lying asleep, flat on the hard bench, with neither pillow nor covering, nor with anyone looking after it. Next, half a dozen men sleeping bolt upright, and leaning against one another in their sleep. In one place a family group, a child asleep in its sleeping mother's arms, and the husband (or male mate) clumsily mending a dilapidated shoe. On another bench a woman trimming the frayed strips of her rags with a knife, and another woman with thread and needle, sewing up rents. Adjoining, a man holding a sleeping woman in his arms. Farther on, a man, his clothing caked with gutter mud, asleep, with his head in the lap of a woman, not more

Social Decay

than twenty-five years old, and also asleep. 'Those women there,' said our guide, 'will sell themselves for thru'pence or tu'pence, or a loaf of stale bread.' He said it with a cheerful sneer."

And then turn back to the preface: "It must not be forgotten that the time of which I write was considered 'good times' in England. The starvation and lack of shelter I encountered constituted a chronic condition of misery, which is never wiped out, even in the periods of greatest prosperity. Following the summer in question came a hard winter. To such an extent did the suffering and positive starvation increase that society was unable to cope with it. Great numbers of the unemployed formed into processions, as many as a dozen at a time, and daily marched through the streets of London crying for bread. Mr. Justin McCarthy, writing in the month of January, 1903, to the New York *Independent*, briefly epitomises the situation, as follows: 'The workhouses have no space left in which to pack the starving crowds who are craving every night at their doors for food and shelter. All the charitable institutions have exhausted their means in trying to raise supplies of food for the famishing residents of the garrets and cellars of London lanes and alleys.'"

And then consider that in the city where

this was going on, the leading newspaper (the *Times*) was printing a three-column article setting forth the fact that competition had grown so great that it was now no longer possible for a "gentleman" to maintain his status with a family in London upon an income of half a million dollars a year!

Yet if one wishes for social contrasts, there is really no need of crossing the ocean. Mr. Schwab's nine million dollar palace in New York will answer the purpose; or so will the St. Regis Hotel. The swinging doors of the St. Regis, so the visitor is informed, cost ten thousand dollars apiece; the panelling of the smoking-room cost forty-five thousand dollars, and the carriage-entrance rain-shed cost eighty-five thousand dollars. The walls of it are covered with a silk brocade, which cost twenty dollars a yard, and the ceiling is gilded with material costing one dollar an ounce. It cost a hundred thousand dollars to fit up the office, and four million dollars to build the whole structure. A two-room apartment in it, without meals, is valued at nine thousand six hundred dollars a year; and for your meals you may try—say, "milk-fed chicken" at two dollars for each tiny portion.

Perhaps this seems monstrous; but it really is not—it is a perfectly inevitable consequence of industrial competition, and of the "constantly increasing mass of

Courtesy of Wilshire's Magazine *From Stereograph, Copyrighted 1906, by Underwood & Underwood*

THE SOCIAL CONTRAST IN NEW YORK

capital." Mr. John Jacob Astor, who owns the hotel, has an income of more than its value every year, and he is in desperate straits to find any way of investing it by which he can make profits. There are seven thousand millionaires in this country, who want the best, the only best they know being what costs the most; and so he knew that if he built a hotel exceeding in cost any other hotel in the world, that hotel would pay him profits. For precisely the same reason a number of buildings are now being torn down in Brooklyn to make room for a graveyard for wealthy people's pet dogs.

The founder of the Astor fortune came to New York a century ago and bought land while it was cheap. Millions of men have since contributed their labour to the building up of New York; and no one of them did anything without adding to the wealth of the Astors—who merely sat by and watched. Now the property of the family is estimated to be worth four hundred and fifty millions of dollars, according to Mr. Burton J. Hendricks's recent account of it in *McClure's Magazine*. It includes half a dozen hotels like the St. Regis; it includes also innumerable slum-tenements with "dark rooms." Its value grows by leaps and bounds—one corner lot on Fifth Avenue "made" them seven hundred thousand dollars in two years. To Mr. William

Waldorf Astor alone the harried and overdriven population of Manhattan Island delivers eight or ten millions of tribute money every year; and Mr. William Waldorf Astor resides at Clieveden, Taplow, Bucks, England—giving as his reason the fact that "America it not a fit place for a gentleman to live in."

The fundamental characteristic of the régime under which we live is that it values a man only in so far as he is capable of producing wealth. Hence one of the signs of the increasing difficulty of making profits will be an increasing recklessness of human life. Our railroads killed six thousand people in 1895, seven thousand in 1899, eight thousand in 1902, nine thousand in 1903, and ten thousand in 1904; they injured thirty-three thousand in 1895, forty-four thousand in 1899, sixty-four thousand in 1902, seventy-six thousand in 1903, and eighty-four thousand in 1904. According to the statistics of the Interstate Commerce Commission, our railways injured one passenger out of every one hundred and eighty-three thousand passengers they carried in 1894; in 1904 they injured one out of every seventy-eight thousand. If casualties are to continue increasing at the same rate until 1912, there are one hundred thousand people under sentence of sudden death, and a number doomed to be maimed greater than

Social Decay

the entire population of the District of Columbia, Delaware, Montana, Arizona, Nevada, Wyoming, Alaska, Idaho and the Hawaiian Islands.

In 1890, before the present appalling slaughter began, we were killing, of a given number of employees, twice as many as the State-owned roads of Germany, and three times as many as Austria. The street railroads of New York City alone take one human life every day, or one in ten thousand of the population every year. People walk about the streets carelessly, but tremble when there is a thunderstorm; yet the street-cars kill ten persons in a year for every one that the lightning kills in the lifetime of a man!

These things create indignation in our pulpits and editorial rooms; but any practical railroad man could tell you that to stop them would be to overthrow society. The reason they occur is that it costs less to pay the damages than it would to take proper precautions, and if the railroads were forced to take the precautions, many of them would have to shut down at once. The situation is covered so completely in the following news item, clipped from the Minneapolis *Journal* of May 26, 1904, that I cannot do better than to quote it entire:

"Because James J. Hill guaranteed eight per cent. to the stockholders of the Burlington when he assumed control of that system, many of the older employees are undergoing what they consider real hardship. Ten days ago the *Journal* voiced the complaints of Burlington employees on other parts of the system, mentioning the fact that the runs to and from the Twin Cities had been combined in some way, to squeeze more work out of the train crews. The new schedule has now been in effect longer and complaints are correspondingly more emphatic. No dissatisfaction is openly expressed, as the Hill guillotine gets nobody more surely than the man who talks too much.

"Trainmen complain that with the long runs and long hours they are forced to work to a point almost beyond human endurance. They are haunted by the fear of accidents from unpreventable neglect of duty. They hold that the running of trains in safety depends upon the vigilance and alertness of the crews and they cannot do themselves and their employers justice, when compelled to work long hours on fast runs.

"Crews are now running from Minneapolis to Chicago, a distance of about 430 miles, with seventy-two stops. The men start from Minneapolis at 7:30 A. M., and arrive, on locals, in Chicago at 9:35 P. M. The men leaving Chicago on No. 50 at 10:50 P. M. arrive in Minneapolis at 1:20 P. M. the next afternoon.

Social Decay 131

"Trainmen declare that in making this schedule the management has broken faith and virtually abrogates previous working agreements. Hints of a strike are made. In discussing the conditions an old Burlington employee said:

" 'A conductor and his crew feel a sense of responsibility for the lives of those upon a train. A man can only be worked so far when he becomes actually irresponsible. I hate to feel that I am in any way responsible for the lives of passengers on a train when the length of the run and hours have worked me beyond my limit. There is no flagman on the train, and the brakeman has to help load baggage, brake, flag, and do anything that comes up. He is certainly not in good condition to be an alert flagman on the latter end of the run.' "*

In the same way it is cheaper for a theatre-manager to bribe police officials with free tickets than to comply with the regulations of the Fire Department; and so it is that five or six hundred people are burned up in

―――――――

* "In the matter of rigging the stock-market the American railroad manager has no superior. In the matter of providing safe and expeditious facilities for transportation he has no inferior in any nation of the first rank. He can manipulate political conventions. He can debauch legislatures. He can send his paid attorneys to Congress and sometimes put them on the bench. In these matters he is a master, just as he is a master in the art of issuing and juggling securities. It is only in the operation of railroads that he is deficient. The mere detail of transporting lives and property safely and satisfactorily he seems to regard as unworthy of his genius. His equipment is usually inadequate. His road-bed is generally second-class or worse. His employees are undisciplined and his system is archaic. Whatever the causes may be, the fact remains that, judged by the results of operation, the American railroad manager is incompetent, and the records of death and disaster prove it."—*New York World.*

five minutes. It is easier to bribe a building inspector than it is to put steel rivets in a building, and so you have a Darlington Hotel collapse, and kill ten or twenty workingmen. And a few weeks later came the *Slocum* disaster, and a helpless steamboat captain was punished, and the responsible capitalists not even named. At the same time, in Trenton, New Jersey, some other capitalists were arrested for making life-preservers with iron bars in them. Of course they were not punished, for everyone understands that such things cannot be helped. In 1893 the number of miners killed in the United States and Canada was two and fifty-three hundredths per thousand; in 1902 it was three and fifty-one hundredths. Better precautions against accidents were one of the demands for making which the miners of Colorado were strung up to telegraph poles, shut in bull-pens, beaten and "deported." Their mortality was thirty-two per thousand in ten years; the mortality among railroad brakemen is now thirty-two per thousand in *two* years, so it was very unreasonable of the miners to complain.

There are annually, says *Social Service*, 344,900 accidents among the 7,086,000 people engaged in this country in manufacturing and mechanical pursuits. It calculates that if the percentage of accidents among

Social Decay   133

the other 23,000,000 employed in other occupations is only one-tenth as much as the above, it means that another 100,000 must be added to the list. "This is perpetual war on humanity," the paper goes on to say, "and more bloody than any civil or international war known to history. This war is costing suffering, physical and mental, which is beyond calculation. It is costing great economic loss. It is creating a sense of wrong and a feeling of class-hatred on the part of those who are its victims."

In the same category of waste of human life belong all the facts of over-driving, long hours, and irregular employment among workingmen. Under the old Southern system of slavery the master took care of his servant the year round; but the wage-slave is kept only while he is needed, and only while he remains at his maximum of working efficiency. Recently in a single month, I clipped from a New York newspaper, items to the effect that the Brooklyn street-railroad combine was discharging all of its superannuated employees; that the master-pilots of the Great Lakes had agreed to engage no man over forty; that the Delaware and Hudson Railroad Company had just published a rule barring all over thirty-five; and that the Carnegie Steel Company had done the same.

And in this same category of waste of

human life belong all the facts of woman and child-labour. For of course the children die; and the women produce deformed and idiot and degenerate offspring, to fill our asylums and prisons. The reader is referred, for first-hand accounts of the life of the American woman wage-slave, to Van Vorst's "The Woman who Toils," and to that fascinating human document, "The Long Day." In Mr. John Spargo's "The Bitter Cry of the Children," he will find a mass of facts about child-labour, the most hideous of all the evils incidental to the process of wealth-concentration.

There is, if one had only time to point it out, no tiniest nook of our society where human lives are not being ground up for profit; the capitalists are ground up, as Mr. Schwab was, and the meanest woman of the town shares his fate. There was a time when a prostitute was an independent person, who could support herself until she grew old; nowadays, under the stress of competition, every city has its prostitution trust. It takes capital to pay the police, and the business is therefore in the hands of the proprietors of houses, who buy young girls out of the slums and immigrant population by thousands and tens of thousands, use them up in a year or two, and then fling them out into the gutters to die, often when they are not out of their

Social Decay

teens. In the same way the gambler and the saloon-keeper are now as much employees as are the officials of the Standard Oil Company: the whole profits of these occupations flowing into the hands of some "captain of industry" as inevitably as all the rills on the mountain-side flow into the river. All of these facts are perfectly familiar, but for the sake of concreteness, I will quote a paragraph from Mr. Steffens's book, "The Shame of the Cities." He is telling of the city of Pittsburg:

"The vice-graft . . . is a legitimate business, conducted, not by the police, but in an orderly fashion by syndicates, and the chairman of one of the parties at the last election, said it was worth two hundred and fifty thousand dollars a year. I saw a man who was laughed at for offering seventeen thousand five hundred dollars for the slot-machine concession; he was told that it was let for much more. 'Speakeasies' (unlicensed drinking places) pay so well that when they earn five hundred dollars or more in twenty-four hours their proprietors often make a bare living. Disorderly houses are managed by ward syndicates. Permission is had from the syndicate real-estate agent, who alone can rent them. The syndicate hires a house from the owners at, say, thirty-five dollars a month, and he lets it to a woman at from thirty-five to fifty dollars a week. For furniture, the tenant must go to the 'official furniture-man,' who delivers one thousand dollars worth of 'fixings' for a note for three thousand dollars, on which high interest must be paid. For beer the tenant must go to the 'official bottler,' and pay two dollars for a one-dollar case of beer; for wines and liquors to the 'official liquor-commissioner,' who charges ten dollars for five dollars' worth; for clothes to the 'official wrapper-maker.' These women may not buy shoes, hats, jewellery, or any other luxury or necessity except from the official concessionaries, and then only at the official, monopoly prices."

And by way of conclusion, in reference to this particular aspect of the consequences of the "increasing mass of capital," let me quote the following little incident, which a friend of mine clipped from one of the New York newspapers:

"One night a young girl called at the entrance to the House of the Good Shepherd in New York City; she asked for food and a place to sleep. 'Twas a pitiful tale she told the matron in charge. She told of her parents having died and left her alone in the great dark city; she told of jobs she had secured but was discharged owing to her physical inability to keep pace with the machine, and as a last resort she appealed to this institution for succour and support. The matron in attendance, after having heard this terrible tale of woe and being thoroughly convinced as to the girl's honesty and integrity, as well as to her virtue, informed her that she could not take her in there, as that institution was established for the reclamation of fallen women only. The poor girl went away, but on the following night she returned. . . . 'You may take me now,' she said, 'you may take me now, for I am a fallen woman!'"

CHAPTER V

BUSINESS AND POLITICS

IN THIS discussion of the process of wealth-concentration, I have so far purposely omitted all mention of the most important aspect of the phenomenon—the seizing by the "constantly increasing mass of capital" of the powers of the State, and their use for purpose of intensifying exploitation. I have avoided that feature, partly because it is conspicuous enough to deserve a chapter to itself, but mainly in order to make clear my view-point, that the phenomenon, while important, is secondary —an effect rather than a cause.

This is, of course, contrary to the view usually taken. In most discussions of the problems of the time, it is taken for granted that "government by special interests" is the source of all the evil. But while recognising how enormously the process of wealth concentration has been accelerated by the political alliance, it is my thesis that exactly the same conditions would have developed had economic forces been left to work out their own results. I maintain that economic competition is a self-destroying stage in social development; and that to regard it as permanent is simply not to realise what it is. For competition is a struggle, and the purpose of every struggle is a victory; to conceive of a struggle without the intention to end the struggle, is simply impossible in the nature of things. In the industrial combat the end is the victory of a class, and the reduction of all other classes to servitude —with the ultimate extinction of all individuals not needed by the victors.

Again, it is generally the custom to regard this phenomenon of class-government with indignation and astonishment, as if it were something abnormal and monstrous; but from the point of view of this discussion, it is a perfectly natural and inevitable incident of the intensification of competition. You are to picture Capital, seeking profits; like a wild beast in a cage, pacing about, watching for an opening, here and there; like water, caught behind a dam, creeping up, crowding forward, feeling for a weak spot. And the one thing to be determined is: *Is there any way in which profits can be made through the powers of government?* If so, it is quite certain that there will be an attempt made by capital to get possession of those powers.

You can see the thing in its germ in any primitive community; I once amused myself by studying it in a little village in Canada, where the trusts had never been heard of. The storekeeper was a rich man, and he had a "pull" with the squire and with the constable and with the game-warden; he did little favours for them, and they for him—so that a poor "Frenchman" who was suspected of stealing a pair of socks found himself in jail before he knew why. And then there was a big "lumber man" in the township; he owned all the jobs, and he traded with the store-keeper, and the storekeeper in return ran the political machine. That was the whole story of the politics of the district—except that there were several fellows of independent temperament, who grumbled, and who constituted the germ of the Socialist movement.

Political corruption first became epidemic in our country in 1861, when the government had to go into business upon an enormous scale. There were contractors—and competition. And then, of course, there was the tariff, a shrewd scheme to compel the people to pay high prices without knowing it. Later on someone discovered the brilliant idea of the franchise, the selling for a nominal sum of the right to tax the public without limit. And so capital went into politics.

At first it did a purely retail business, buying up the legislators as it needed them; but soon the thing became systematised, and Capital got wholesale prices—it financed the machines, and chose its own candidates. The process culminated at the beginning of the present decade, when "big business" was in practically undisputed possession of both the majority parties, of Congress and the Presidency, and of the governments in every town, city and state in America.

You see, it was as if our society was in unstable equilibrium. We had a political democracy, and we were developing an industrial aristocracy; and it was impossible for them to exist side by side. Innocent people had taken it for granted that they could; but it is no more possible for a democracy to be aristocratic in any of its aspects and remain a democracy, than it is for a virtuous man to be vicious in one particular, and remain a virtuous man. Democracy is not a code of laws, nor is it a system of government—it is an attitude of soul. It has as its basis a perception of the spiritual nature of man, from which follows the corollary that all men either are equal, or must become so. And so between aristocracy and democracy, wherever and under whatever aspects they appear, there is, and forever must be, eternal and deadly war. Here is the testimony and the warning of the greatest of American democrats, Abraham Lincoln, who if he could rise from his grave to speak to us in these times of our country's trial could speak no more pertinent words than these. He had declared that the Slavery question was one between right and wrong. "Right and wrong," he said—"that is the issue that will continue in this country when these poor tongues of Judge Douglas and myself shall be silent. It is the eternal struggle between these two principles—right and wrong—throughout the world. They are the principles which have stood face to face from the beginning of time and will ever continue to struggle. The one is the common right of humanity, and the other is the divine right of kings. It is the same principle in whatever shape it develops itself. It is the same spirit that says: 'You work and toil and earn bread, and I'll eat it.' No matter in what shape it comes, whether from the mouth of a king who seeks to bestride the people of his own nation, and live by the fruit of their labour, or from one race of men as an apology for enslaving another race, it is the same tyrannical principle."

It is worth while pointing out the utter hopelessness of the struggle. On the one hand was the capitalist, with his millions, alert, aggressive and resourceful; he had an army of experts to help him—shrewd attorneys, skilful lobbyists, newspapers and publicity bureaus, political henchmen trained all their lifetime to the trade; he was cold and unscrupulous—as a rule he

Business and Politics

was not a man at all, but a corporation, a thing without a soul, a monster "clamouring for dividends." He had a thousand devices, a thousand pretences, a thousand disguises. And opposed to him was the Public—unorganised, uninformed, and sound asleep!

Recently, when Mr. H. G. Wells was in this country, I had a long talk with him, and he asked me how I accounted for the saturnalia of corruption in our political life; he said that our people did not seem to him degraded or brutal, and he could not understand why things were so much worse here than in England. I said that in England the economic process had been modified by the existence of an hereditary aristocracy, holding over from old times and having high traditions of public service. By nature this aristocracy sympathised with capital, and to a certain extent fraternised with it; but it would not abdicate to it, and occasionally, to preserve its own power, it made concessions to the public, and so served as a check upon the forces of commercialism. On the other hand the American people had only themselves to rely upon and until they had been goaded into revolt, there was no limit whatever to the power of greed.

I suppose it is unnecessary to offer any proofs of the existence of "government by special interests." If there is anyone who has been out of the country for the past three years and has not read any of the magazines, it will be sufficient to refer him to the two books of Mr. Lincoln Steffens—"The Shame of the Cities" and "The Struggle for Self Government."

Mr. Steffens himself is a proof of the evil conditions: a man who has spent ten years studying our politics, who went to the task with no preconceptions, and only a passion for honesty and fair dealing—and who has been made into a thorough-going radical by the irresistible logic of facts. It was his particular service to the Republic to trace the stream of graft to its fountain-head, which is what he calls "big-business"; and the series of papers in which he proved that thesis to our people will long be studied as models of the higher journalism—the journalism which is to ordinary newspaper writing what statesmanship is to politics.

As I say, there is no need of proof; but simply by way of illustration, and to call the picture to the reader's mind, let me quote a few paragraphs from one of these papers—"Pittsburg, a City Ashamed":

"The railroads began the corruption of this city. There always was some dishonesty, as the oldest public men I talked with said, but it was occasional and criminal till the first great corporation made it business-like and respectable. The Pennsylvania Railroad was in the system from the start, and as the other roads came in and found the city government bought up by those before them, they purchased their rights of way by outbribing the older roads, then joined the ring to acquire more rights for themselves and to keep belated rivals out. As corporations multiplied and capital branched out, corruption increased naturally, but the notable characteristic of the 'Pittsburg plan' of misgovernment was that it was not a haphazard growth, but a deliberate, intelligent organisation. . . . The Pennsylvania Railroad is a power in Pennsylvania politics, it is part of the State ring, and part also of the Pittsburg ring. The city paid in all sorts of rights and privileges, streets, bridges, etc., and in certain periods the business interests of the city were sacrificed to leave the Pennsylvania road in exclusive control of a freight traffic it could not handle alone."

The "bosses" who ruled Pittsburg were Magee and Flynn, and Mr. Steffens prints in full the agreement between them and Senator Quay, by which they divided the boodle of the state. "Magee and Flynn were the government and the law. How could they commit a crime? If they wanted something from the city they passed an ordinance granting it, and if some other ordinance was in conflict it was repealed or amended. If the laws of the state stood in the way, so much the worse for the laws of the state; they were amended. If the constitution of the state proved a barrier, as it did to all special legislation, the Legislature enacted a law for cities of the second class (which was Pittsburg alone) and the courts upheld the Legislature. If there were opposition on the side of public opinion, there was a use for that also.

"As I have said before, unlawful acts were exceptional and unnecessary in Pittsburg. Magee did not steal franchises and sell them. His councils gave them to him. He and the busy Flynn took them, and built railways, which Magee sold and bought and financed and conducted, like any other man whose successful career is held up as an example for young men. His railways, combined into the Consolidated Traction Company, were capitalised at thirty million dollars. There was scandal in Chicago over the granting of charters for twenty-eight and fifty years. Magee's read, 'for nine hundred and fifty years,' 'for nine hundred and ninety-nine years,' 'said Charter is to exist a thousand years,' 'said Charter is to exist perpetually,' and the Councils gave franchises for the 'life of the charter.'"

And all this was a regular profession, a custom of the country, which its devotees

Business and Politics

studied. "Two of them told me repeatedly that they travelled about the country looking up the business, and that a fellowship had grown up among boodling aldermen of the leading cities in the United States. Committees from Chicago would come to St. Louis to find out what 'new games' the St. Louis boodlers had, and they gave the St. Louisans hints as to how they 'did the business' in Chicago. So the Chicago and St. Louis boodlers used to visit Cleveland and Pittsburg and all the other cities, or, if the distance was too great, they got their ideas by those mysterious channels which run all through the 'World of Graft.' The meeting place in St. Louis was Decker's stable, and ideas unfolded there were developed into plans which the boodlers say to-day, are only in abeyance. In Decker's stable was born the plan to sell the Union Market; and though the deal did not go through, the boodlers, when they saw it failing, made the market-men pay ten thousand dollars for killing it. This scheme is laid aside for the future. Another that failed was to sell the court-house, and this was well under way when it was discovered that the ground on which this public building stands was given to the city on condition that it was to be used for a court-house and nothing else. . . . The grandest idea of all came from Philadelphia. In that city the gas-works were sold out to a private concern, and the water-works were to be sold next. The St. Louis fellows have been trying ever since to find a purchaser for their waterworks. The plant is worth at least forty million dollars. But the boodlers thought they could let it go at fifteen million dollars, and get one million dollars or so themselves for the bargain. 'The scheme was to do it and skip,' said one of the boodlers who told me about it, 'and if you could mix it all up with some filtering scheme it could be done. Only some of us thought we could make more than one million dollars out of it—a fortune apiece. It will be done some day.' . . .

"Such, then, is the boodling system as we see it in St. Louis. Everything the city owned was for sale by the officers elected by the people. The purchasers might be willing or unwilling takers; they might be citizens or outsiders; it was all one to the city government. So long as the members of the combines got the proceeds they would sell out the town. Would? They did and they will. If a city treasurer runs away with fifty thousand dollars there is a great halloo about it. In St. Louis the regularly organised thieves who rule have sold fifty million dollars' worth of franchises and other valuable municipal assets. This is the estimate made for me by a banker, who

Business and Politics 149

said that the boodlers got not one-tenth of the value of the things they sold."

Two or three years ago, before I met Mr. Steffens, I thought that he knew only as much as he "let on"; and so I wrote him an "open letter," to point out the consequences of this régime of "big business." The story of this manuscript is an amusing one, and worth telling for the light it throws upon my argument. Mr. Steffens was so good as to say that it was the best criticism of himself that he had ever read; and it was scheduled for publication in one of our three or four largest magazines. But alas— it was purchased by the enthusiastic young editor, and then read by the elderly and unenthusiastic proprietor. When I rebelled at the long wait which followed, the proprietor invited me to dinner, and unbosomed his soul to me. He was the dearest old gentleman I ever met, and he put his arm about me while he explained the situation. "My boy," he said, "you are a very clever chap, and you know a lot; but why don't you put it all into a book, where you can't hurt anyone but yourself? Why do you try to get it into my magazine, and scare away my half-million subscribers?"

So the letter was shelved. But the questions it asked are now the questions which events are asking of the American people; and so I shall take the advice of the elderly and unenthusiastic proprietor—and publish some of the letter in a book! It ran as follows:

This is the question I have wished to ask you, Mr. Steffens. "A revolution has happened," you tell us; we have no longer "a government of the people, by the people, for the people,"—we have "a government of the people, by the rascals, for the rich." And if we find that that revolution, which has overthrown the law, and which defies the law, cannot be put down and overcome by the means of the law—what are we going to do then? Are we going to sit still, and content ourselves with saying it is too bad? Are we going to bear it—to bear it forever? *Can* we bear it forever? And if we cannot bear it forever what are we going to do when we can bear it no longer?

A revolution is a serious thing, Mr. Steffens. A man should not talk about a "revolution" except with a thorough realisation of what the word implies. A revolution means that the social contract has been broken, that rights have been violated and justice defied—that, in a word, the game of life has not been fairly played, that those who have lost may possibly have had the right to win. And the game of life is a pretty stern game for many of us, Mr. Steffens.

Business and Politics

You and your friends, I and my friends, belong to a class whom this "system" touches only through our ideals. Editors and authors, clergymen and lawyers, we are pained to know that corruption is eating out the heart of our country—but still, if the problem be not solved to-day, we can put it off till to-morrow, and not realise what a difference it makes. But there are some in our country whom the System touches far more intimately and directly than this— some to whom the difference between to-day and to-morrow is simply a difference between life and death. I happened only yesterday to be reading a letter from a man who, I think, knows that "System," which is our new government, in this personal and intimate way. I will quote a few words from his letter:

"I have been arrested, put in jail, prosecuted and persecuted. I have had my customers driven away; I have been boycotted to the extent that men who dared to trade with me have lost their jobs; I have had my home broken into at night; been beaten with guns and abused by vile and foul-mouthed thugs; been torn, partly dressed and bleeding, from the side of my wife, who was driven from her bedroom and roughly handled; and finally I have been shipped out and told that if I returned to my home I would be hung. Not satisfied with this they have twice deported my brother, who was conducting the business in which we were both earning our living, so that it became necessary for an adjuster to take charge of our store." All this was, needless to say, in Colorado; the writer is Mr. A. H. Floaten, a storekeeper of Telluride, but now of Richmond County, Wisconsin, where he was working in a hayfield when he wrote. He goes on to add that the charge upon which he was "deported" was that of selling goods to members of the Western Federation of Miners. "As for my brother and myself," he states, "I defy any and all persons to show a single instance where either of us have ever violated any law or even been suspected of crime, or have ever wronged any person."

Here is your "revolution," Mr. Steffens, in full swing. One of the questions which I have for some months found myself longing to ask you is, how clearly you recognised in the Colorado civil war the natural and inevitable consequences of a continuation of your "government of the people, by the rascals, for the rich?" Here is an unequivocal declaration, by a vote of two to one, by the people in one of the states of this free country, in favour of a constitutional amendment permitting an eight-hour law; and here are representatives of both the majority parties pledging themselves to enact it, and then openly and shamelessly selling themselves out to the predatory corporations of the state. The people then resort to a strike to secure their rights; and when they are seen to be winning, the militia is summoned, criminals are hired to commit a dynamite outrage and afford the necessary pretext, and then every tradition of American liberty and every safeguard of free institutions is overthrown, and the strike crushed and the striker's organisation exterminated with a ruthlessness and a recklessness which no police official in Russia could have surpassed. And then the party of "law and order"—that is the "System"—sat enthroned in Colorado, and the guileless reader of newspaper despatches believed that an "election" took place in that state last November! The "System" suspended the *Habeas Corpus* Act, censored newspapers and telegrams, opened mails, entered houses without warrant and drove women from their beds at dead of night, deported men, defied and threatened judges, shut down mines in spite of their owners' will—and finally haled a score or two of elected officials before it and put ropes around their necks and compelled them to resign. And then the "rebellion," that is, the agitation for an eight-hour law, attempted to reassert itself in the form of ballots; and by means of a threat of deposition it compelled the newly elected governor to accede in everything to its will—and in particular to retain in office the infamous militia official who was its agent in these crimes!

But we, as I said before, are touched by these things only through our ideals. We are sorry to see American institutions overthrown in an American state; but we do not live in Colorado, and we are quite sure that there is no danger of our being turned out of our homes. And yet we know that the system exists in our own city and state, and sits just as surely intrenched there as in Colorado. And we know also that it exists for a purpose—that it exists to rule. And are we to imagine that it exists to rule the people of Patagonia, of Greenland and Afghanistan? Do we not know that it exists to rule *us*?

How does it rule us? How does it rule the people of Colorado? Whatever is it that is wanted of the people of Colorado? Why, simply that they should go into the mines and factories and work, not eight hours a day, as they wished to, but twelve hours a day, the time the "System" bade them to. And what is it that it wants everywhere else—in California, in Maine and in Texas? What, save that those who have labour to sell shall sell it at the price the "System" is paying, and that those who have goods to buy shall buy them at the price the "System"

Business and Politics 155

asks? If this be so, is not the only difference between us and the people of Colorado that they went on strike against the "System," whereas we are not on strike—we *pay?*

Let us deal with facts. Here is a corporation which runs a street-railroad in a city. It gives an abominable service, its cars are cold and filthy, its employees are underpaid wretches who work thirteen and fifteen hours a day—and the fare is just double that of the splendid government service of Berlin. And the public-spirited men of the city have for ten or twenty years been trying to do something with that corporation at the state capital; but the corporation has its lobby and continues to pay big dividends upon its watered stock year after year. And then do the people of the city organise and go on strike against that corporation? No indeed—they pay.

You know of the agitation for a parcels post; you know that under the parcels-post system an Englishman can send a package to California for one-third of what it costs us to send one from New York. In Germany a ten-pound package may be sent anywhere in the Empire for twelve cents; and our post office pays the railroads more for its service than all the rest of the civilised world combined, though the quantity of mail matter carried is less than that of

Great Britain, France and Germany alone! Yet we know that it is a waste of ink setting these facts forth. Is not the president of the United States Express Company the United States senator from your own state? The railroad systems of this country have, of course, their lobby in every state capital, and in Washington as well; and every single year the railroad systems of this country slaughter and maim the equivalent of a Gettysburg campaign—there were as many people killed in the last three years as the British lost in the entire Boer war. Yet there is not the least reason for this; the railroads could, if they chose, build cars which will not crumble up like matchboxes— they have proven it by killing only six Pullman-car passengers in the same three years. But of course you have to pay a large sum extra to ride in a Pullman car. If you cannot pay with money, you pay with your bones—in either case, of course, you pay.

And then there is the tariff. You, Mr. Steffens, are a man who has both the ability and the honesty to think, and you know what the tariff is. You know that it is a device to keep out foreign competition and thus enable home manufacturers to charge higher prices. You know that in the early days its effect was to make manufacturing possible by keeping prices at a level where a fair profit was paid. Above this level they could not go, because there was free domestic competition. The tariff was thus a tax, self-imposed by every man in the country, for the purpose of building up the country's home industries; exactly as if the owner of a sugar-plantation should conclude it would pay him to grind his own cane, and should set aside his gains for a few years to buy the machinery. Now I might stop to argue the socialistic implications of such a procedure—involving as it does the doctrine that the manufactures are the interest and concern of the whole people, to the advantages of which, when completed, they all have a right. (No plantation master, I take it, would expect to furnish himself with machinery out of the wages of his hands.) Continuing, however, to discuss facts and not theories, you see that these industries which we have "encouraged" have now become the mightiest power in the land. It is they who have accomplished the revolution and set up the "System"; it is they who use the money which the people have turned over to them, to maintain and perpetuate the old arrangement—an arrangement which now enables them, since they have become monopolies, to charge for their products from thirty to fifty per cent. more than a fair price, as is proven by what they charge abroad.

The workingman, you know, Mr. Steffens, has all this justified to him by the fact that he gets his share of this "prosperity"; but of late the workingman has been finding that he does *not* get his share. He has brought the industrial machinery of the country to such a pitch of perfection that he produces more than the country needs; and so when foreign markets fail he is out of work part of the time; and the mass of unemployed labour operates by the "iron law" to beat down wages and to break strikes, and to make his share less and less. And all the time, to pay interest on the constantly increasing capital of the country, the prices of trust products are being raised yet higher, and the cost of living is rising, year by year.

In the cotton mills of Alabama and Georgia little children six and eight years of age are working twelve hours for a wage of nine cents a day. And how do you think they fare in this fearful race for profits —what do you think is the effect upon them of the continued operation of the "System"? You may remember that I said a little way back that there were people in this country to whom the difference between to-day and to-morrow is simply a difference between life and death. It was such people as these I had in mind.

Look, Mr. Steffens; you go from town to

Business and Politics 159

city, and from city to state, and everywhere you show us hordes of political parasites battening on corruption; and you tell us that the fortunes that they make represent but a small portion of what is made by the "big business-men" who bribe them. Magee and Quay, you tell us, made thirty millions out of the street railroads of Pittsburg; and all over this land, year in and year out, such sums are being "made." And soon afterward came Mr. Lawson's story of how the Standard Oil group "made" forty-six million dollars in a single deal without turning over their hands. Mr. Lawson expatiates upon this way of "making" dollars—he makes reflections which I had often wondered if you were making. I have wondered if you realised entirely that these millions of dollars were *real* dollars? Dollars that a man might spend, just the same as any other dollars—with which he might purchase food that men had toiled to raise, and houses that men had toiled to build! I am writing these words in October, and the windows of my room look out upon a cornfield. All the year long I have watched a farmer and his son at work in this field—first plowing it, then harrowing it back and forth and across, then planting the corn, patiently, row by row. The field is ten acres in size, and it seemed to me that not a week passed all summer that the farmer was not plowing and weeding it; and now that the fall has come he has cut it stalk by stalk, and stacked it; and now I can see him and his son sitting on the bare, bleak hillside this morning, husking it, ear by ear. That will take them all of two or three weeks, and when the whole thing has been done they will gather up the ears to cart them to town, and the farmer will have five hundred bushels of corn and will get for them two hundred and fifty dollars. And then I read Mr. Lawson's account of how the Rockefellers "made" forty-six million dollars out of Amalgamated Copper —and strive to realise that what they made was the equivalent of the labour of the farmer and the farmer's sons and the farmer's horses in one hundred and eighty-six thousand ten-acre cornfields such as the one I look out upon!

Is it not obvious that if I were to have the power to call a piece of paper one dollar and to put it into circulation, exchanging it for two bushels of corn, I could only do it by diminishing the value of every other dollar in the country a certain small amount? Supposing that the total wealth of the country was one billion dollars, I should diminish every single dollar by one-billionth. Suppose that similarly I "made" one million dollars—by any sort of "making" whatever save by producing some useful thing and increasing the total wealth of the country—I should then tax the holder of every dollar one mill. A man who owned ten thousand dollars would be robbed by me of ten dollars—he would be robbed of it just as literally and as actually as if I had broken into his house and stolen his watch, He would not know that he was robbed, perhaps—all that he would know would be that when he spent his ten thousand dollars he would not get quite so much. In Dun's and Bradstreet's the event would be recorded in the statement that the cost of living had risen one-tenth of one per cent. since last week, and that interest rates had similarly declined. And now here is the young girl who works in the sweatshops of Chicago for a wage of forty cents a week, as thousands of them do. The great Amalgamated Copper deal is consummated, Mr. Rockefeller and his fellow-conspirators "make" forty-six million dollars—and the young girl's wage becomes thirty-nine cents and a fraction. At forty cents she was hanging on for her life; at thirty-nine cents and a fraction she enters the nearest brothel. Here is the little child of eight years toiling from six at night till six in the morning in the midst of throbbing cotton-looms for nine cents. Magee and Quay of Pittsburg "make" thirty million dollars in street railroads—and the little child's wage becomes eight cents and a fraction. At nine cents he was starving; at eight and a fraction he faints, and the machinery seizes him, and his arm has been torn out of him before anyone can answer his screams. So it is, Mr. Steffens, that there are people in this country to whom the difference between to-day and to-morrow is simply a difference between life and death.

That farmer about whose work I spoke will take his two hundred and fifty dollars to the bank for deposit; and in the line before the window will be a young spendthrift idler with a month's income from his father's estate, and a politician with a bribe for a street railway franchise; and to the banker all these deposits will stand upon equal terms, they will all be equally "good," and will claim and get interest at the same rate. The farmer will have to content himself with a lower rate, because of the competition of the others; and next week, when the activities of some speculator in Wall Street bring about a failure of the bank, he will get not a bit more out of the wreck than the other two. And then he will go back and toil for another year, to raise a similar crop—and what will he find then? Why this: the forty-six millions of the Standard Oil gang will have survived all mischances, and having by their enormous mass attracted profits, will have

Business and Politics   163

become fifty millions, or even sixty; and the thirty millions of Magee and Quay will have become thirty-five. All the untold millions of the capital of the country will have increased similarly; and the investment field will have become more crowded yet, and the prizes fewer yet, and the chances more hazardous yet; and the cost of living will be a little higher yet; and the interest rate a little lower yet, and wages a little lower yet; and the whole of human society will be toiling a little harder yet to pay the profits upon that heaped-up mass of wealth. More men will be taking to drink, and more women will be taking to brothels—more to suicide, madness, vagabondage and crime. The race for profits will be a little more fierce, social ostentation will be a little more vulgar, political corruption will be a little more shameless, strikes and riots will be a little more common, the socialists will be a little more active—and you, Mr. Lincoln Steffens, will be a little more saddened at the sight of your country's downward career.

I have noticed the very curious fact about your views, that all your hope of betterment is in the future—it is always how we can prevent new stealing, never how we can punish the past. And so those thirty million dollars of Magee and Quay, the forty-six millions of the Amalgamated deal—they are safe and beyond recall forever?

Mr. Lawson talks about "restitution"; do do you think he will ever bring it about—do you see any signs of it so far? And yet those forty-six million dollars, assuming that they grow at ten per cent., a small earning for such a sum—year after year they will be, roughly speaking, as follows: 46, 51, 56, 63, 69, 76, 84, 92, 101, 111, 122, 134, 147, 162, 178, 196, 216, 238, 262, 288, 318, and so on. In other words, the heirs of the "Amalgamated" financiers will twenty years from now have multiplied that sum nearly seven times, and be receiving nearly seven times as much tribute from the sewing-girl in the Chicago slums and the children in the Georgia cotton mill. I, Mr. Steffens, am one of those who look upon all profits, rent, interest, and dividends as a survival of barbarism, the last but not the least of the devices whereby the strong enslave the weak and profit by their toil; but I assume that you are not one of these—that you are one of the class I heard described by a speaker the other night, "who think that the first dollar is a male dollar and the second a female, and that when you put them in the bank together they bring forth dimes and nickels, which in the course of the years grow up to be dollars as big as their parents." Yet even so, you can not but recognise the distinction between legitimate and illegitimate children. You can

not—to drop an inconvenient metaphor—
claim that society can by any possibility
whatever be required to go on paying tribute
to that stolen forty-six millions—the three
hundred and eighteen millions of twenty
years from now. It is a maxim of law, Mr.
Steffens, that there is no wrong without its
redress.

And if you grant this and begin to examine the millions in that light—what
perplexities you come upon! Only take the
tariff, for instance—is there a dollar invested
in the business of this country to-day which
has not profited by that, and which is therefore not made up out of the tiny contributions of thousands of persons who not
only do not own that dollar, but do not own
any other dollar? And then consider that
the beginnings of most of our great fortunes
were made in Civil War times, when the
nation in its extremity paid two dollars for
every dollar in value it received! And consider the chaos of political corruption that
followed, the twenty years of plundering of
every variety that American ingenuity could
invent, from Black Friday to the Western
land grabs and railroad steals! Try to
figure how many crimes are represented by
the Vanderbilt millions, how many by the
Goulds's; think of the commercial assassinations represented by the word Standard
Oil—the secret rebates and discriminations,

the wholesale buyings of legislatures and elections; think of the whole institution of corruption of the present day, of the "System," intrenched in village and town, city, and state, and nation, owning both parties, the executive, the legislative, and the judicial branches of the Government, the schools, the colleges, the pulpits, the press, literature, and art, and public opinion—making it, not figuratively and hyperbolically, but literally, simply, and indisputably the fact that there is not to-day in the land a place where a man can take a dollar and invest it, and get back a copper cent that is not tainted with corruption, polluted by violence, treason, and crime, and stained with the blood and tears of uncounted thousands of agonised women and children!

So much for the letter. If there is anyone who, after reading it, is still of the opinion that the people should pay the tribute demanded twenty years from now, there is nothing more that I can say to him—except to give a few statistics by way of further elucidation, showing him how many more millions of dollars there will be to enter their claim. There will be, for instance, the four hundred and fifty million dollars of the Astor family—all invested in New York City real estate, and at the rate of growth of the city, certainly destined to be a billion

Business and Politics 167

dollars in twenty years from date. There is the half billion dollars of Mr. Rockefeller, increasing by a most conservative estimate at the rate of ten per cent. per year, and therefore destined to be over four billions at that time. And then there are the railroads of the country. We are now being prepared for a decision to be some day delivered by the Supreme Court, to the effect that any rate regulation which interferes with dividends is confiscation, and therefore unconstitutional. And yet we know that railroad capitalisation is simply a function of earning-power; that what the financiers have uniformly done was to charge all the traffic would bear, and then water their stock until the rate of dividends came down to the market average. The capitalisation of the railroads of the country, fixed upon this basis, is thirteen billion dollars, whereas their actual cost was only six or seven billions. To give one or two samples of this process, the Western Maryland Railroad was bought up by the Goulds, and watered from nine millions up to fifty-one millions. The Central Railroad of Georgia, which cost less than seven millions, has now been watered up to fifty-five millions. Assuming that the watering were to stop to-day, and that the railroads simply re-invested their dividends at the present rate of six per cent., in twenty years we should be paying interest upon over forty billion dollars.

From a brokerage circular which recently came in my mail, I have clipped a few more instances of the workings of trust finance. The argument of the circular is that I need not be frightened at their offer to make my money earn more than six per cent.—that over a hundred per cent. is "being frequently earned by legitimate business." Thus the Diamond Match Company recently paid ten per cent. on a capitalisation of fifteen million dollars, when its original capitalisation had been only six million dollars. The Western Union Telegraph Company began in 1858 with only three hundred and eighty-five thousand dollars, yet in 1874 it paid one hundred and fourteen per cent. on seventeen million dollars. Anyone who had invested one thousand dollars in this stock in 1858 would by 1890 have received fifty thousand dollars in stock dividends and one hundred thousand dollars in cash dividends. The present capital is over ninety-seven millions—"and the greater part of the equipment has been created out of the earnings of the company!" In the case of the Prudential Life Insurance Company (owing, though the circular does not state it, to a little deal between United States Senator Dryden and the New Jersey State Legislature) for every one thousand dollars originally paid in, the stockholders now own twenty-two thousand dollars' worth of stock and received annual cash dividends of twenty-two hundred dollars, or two hundred and twenty per cent. upon their original investment! And then, to diversify the subject, let us consider the tariff, and its variegated plunderings. In a letter to the New York *Evening Post* of Oct. 26th, 1904, Mr. J. R. Dunlap gave some figures showing the "scandalous taxes imposed by trusts upon the people":

"Now, to show how the Dingley duty of eight dollars per ton on steel rails taxes American railroads and hence reaches deep into the pockets of shippers and travellers on American railroads, I need only cite the fact that, during the year 1903 our American railroads purchased from the steel pool exactly three million forty-six thousand eight hundred and thirty-six tons of new steel rails (see statistical abstract, Department of Commerce and Labour). The price to *foreign* railroads being, say twenty dollars per ton—as we *now know*—and the pool price to American railroads being twenty-eight dollars per ton, that means that the American people, *during the single year last past*, contributed a clean net profit of twenty-four million three hundred and seventy-four thousand six hundred and eighty-eight dollars to the rail pool—by reason, presumably, of their "patriotic" belief in the Dingley duties! And during the past six years—since the Dingley Bill was enacted—these same American railroads have been forced to contribute to the few members of the rail pool exactly one hundred and two million six hundred and twenty-one thousand two hundred and fifty-six dollars, or eight dollars per ton on twelve million eight hundred and twenty-seven thousand six hundred and fifty-seven tons of rails bought and used. Dividing that stupendous sum of protection profit (one hundred and two million six hundred and twenty-one thousand two hundred and fifty-six dollars) by eighty million of population, we see that the rail pool alone—to say nothing of other combinations "sheltered" by the Dingley duties—has collected a tax of exactly one dollar and twenty-eight and one-quarter cents (1.28\frac{1}{4}$) for every man, woman, and child in America, white and coloured.

"To further indicate the fabulous profits which the Dingley duties make possible to our 'infant' iron and steel industries, I need only cite recent and familiar records. In the spring of 1899, when the Steel Trust was in process of formation, and when it became necessary for the influential men in the steel industry to *prove* what enormous profits the steel manufacturers were making,

Business and Politics 171

and thus to induce the investing public to put their money into Steel Trust stocks— then it was that Mr. Charles M. Schwab, president, wrote to Mr. Henry C. Frick, chairman of the Carnegie Steel Company, the famous letter of May 15, 1899, now public property, in which Mr. Schwab used these words:'

" 'What is true of rails *is equally true of other steel products*. . . . *You know* we can make rails for less than twelve dollars per ton, leaving a nice margin on foreign business.'

"Mark you, that was in 1899, when the boom was at its zenith, when wages were highest, and when all the costs of production were far above all averages of recent boom years.

"To show how accurate Mr. Schwab was in these statements, and to show how trustworthy was his confident forecast of future profits, I need only cite the following speaking figures from the two annual statements which have been made public by the United States Steel Corporation, namely:

Total number of employees:
   1902.   1903.
  168,127 167,709
Total annual salaries and wages paid:
  $120,528,343.00 $120,763,896.00
Net earnings:
  $133,308,763.72 $109,171,152.35

"It will be observed that during these two years the average annual net earnings of the Steel Trust *exceeded the total labour cost of their entire product!*

MEDICINAL PRODUCTS

"Turning from the iron and steel industry, we might take quinine, and many other medicinal products; we might take chemicals, many of them most essential in manufacturing industry; we might take borax, which sells in America at seven and one-half cents per pound, and in Britain at two and one-half cents per pound, because the Dingley duty is exactly five cents per pound; we might take mica, a mining product largely used in the electrical, wall-paper and stove-making industries, and which enjoys a modest protection ranging from one hundred and fifty to four thousand per cent. In short, we might take each and every staple product now made in America, and needlessly sheltered by the Dingley duties, and prove, by comparative prices at home and abroad, that the fabulous profits which the gentlemen engaged in these industries are now making—and which they have capitalised into watered "industrials" —are due chiefly and directly to the fostering care of the Dingley Bill, which was designed to protect our 'infant' industries."

Business and Politics 173

In the same issue, another correspondent, Mr. W. J. Gibson, shows how the Government serves as a tool of the trusts in tariff exactions. He gives several columns of facts about such outrages as the "Rupee Cases," For instance:

"There have been nine or ten decisions on this one question against the Government, and still the secretary of the treasury refuses to refund the money which the courts have decided so often he has exacted illegally. The money he has directed to be wrongfully assessed and collected, and is retaining in these cases, known as "the Rupee Cases," amounts to over a million dollars. The parties cannot get any interest for their money so wrongfully withheld, and the customs officials are still being directed to assess all merchandise coming from India on the basis of the rupee at the value of thirty-two cents in our money. This has gone on for more than six years, and against the decision of the United States Circuit Court since January 7, 1899."

And now, can we get any broad view of the results of this long process of wealth-concentration? In 1850 the wealth of the United States was estimated at nine billions; in 1870 it was thirty billions; in 1890 it was sixty-five billions; and in 1900 it was ninety-five billions. How is this wealth distributed? Writing in 1896, Dr. C. B.

Spahr made his famous calculation, embodied in the statement that one-eighth of the population owned seven-eighths of the wealth, and that one per cent. owned more than the remaining ninety-nine per cent. And at that time the machinery of exploitation had hardly more than got under way. The best attempt at an estimate since then is the one by Lucien Sanial, published by the American Branch of the International Institute of Social Science. This is the result of a careful analysis of the census of 1900; it shows that of ninety-five billions of the country's present wealth, sixty-seven billions are owned by a capitalist-class of two hundred and fifty thousand persons, twenty-four billions by a middle-class of eight million four hundred thousand persons, and four billions by a working-class of over twenty million persons. And now, if the sixty-seven billions owned by the capitalists be assumed to earn ten per cent.—which is surely a reasonable average amount—our people will be paying interest upon four hundred and fifty billion dollars at the end of the twenty year period!

And that represents the centralisation of the actual ownership of wealth; but one does not get a real understanding of the situation until he begins to consider the centralisation of the *control* of wealth. In explaining the struggle over the surplus

Business and Politics 175

of the life-insurance companies, one of our financial magnates remarked to me: "I would rather have the power of manipulating four hundred million dollars, than the actual ownership of fifty millions." And with that crucial fact in mind, let one consider the figures given by Mr. Sereno S. Pratt in *The World's Work* for December, 1903, and summarised in Dr. Strong's "Social Progress," as follows:

"One-twelfth of the estimated wealth of the United States is represented at the meeting of the Board of Directors of the United States Steel Corporation.

"They represent as influential directors more than two hundred other companies. These companies operate nearly one-half of the railroad mileage of the United States. They are the great miners and carriers of coal. The leading telegraph system, the traction lines of New York, of Philadelphia, of Pittsburg, of Buffalo, of Chicago, and of Milwaukee, and one of the principal express companies, are represented in the board. This group includes also directors of five insurance companies, two of which have assets of seven hundred millions of dollars. In the Steel Board are men who speak for five banks and ten trust companies in New York City, including the First National, the National City, and the Bank of Commerce, the three greatest banks in the country, and the heads of important chains of financial institutions. Telephone, electric, real estate, cable, and publishing companies are represented there, and our greatest merchant sits at the board table.

"What the individual wealth of these men is, it would be impossible and beside the point to estimate; but one of them, Mr. John D. Rockefeller, is generally estimated to be the richest individual in the world. But it is not the personal, but the representative, wealth of those men that makes the group extraordinary. They control corporations whose capitalisations aggregate more than nine billion dollars—an amount (if the capitalisations are real values) equal to about the combined public debts of Great Britain, France, and the United States. It is this concentration of power which is significant. There were at the time of the last statement sixty-nine thousand nine hundred and fifty-five stockholders in the Steel Corporation. But the control of this corporation is vested in twenty-four directors, and this board of directors is guided by the executive and finance committees, which in turn are largely directed by their chairmen, who are probably selected by the great banker who organised the corporation and in a large part sways its policy.

"Examinations show that the concentration of control of these great New York

Business and Politics 177

City banks has gone so far that a comparatively small group of capitalists possesses the power to regulate the flow of credit in this country. In the last analysis it is found that there are actually only two main influences, and that these are centred in Mr. Morgan and Mr. Rockefeller. It is possible to express in approximate figures the extent of the Morgan influence"— which the writer shows in a table to figure up over six billion two hundred and sixty-eight million dollars. How very conservative is Mr. Pratt's estimate is shown by the fact that he gives the number of holders of shares of the railroads of this country as nine hundred and fifty thousand persons; with which the reader may contrast the following editorial paragraph from a recent issue of the New York *Times:*

"It would appear from evidence collected by the Interstate Commerce Commission and communicated to the Senate, that the ownership of the railroad system of this country is not as widely diffused as has been supposed. On the 30th of June, 1904, the 1,220 railroads reporting to the Commission had only 327,851 stockholders of record. This total includes many duplications, as it was impossible to know in how many instances one capitalist was represented in the stockholding interest of several railroads. Assuming the population of the United

States to be, in round figures, eighty millions, the entire mileage of the railroads doing an interstate business is owned by about four-tenths of 1 per cent. of the people of this country."

Such is the situation. It completes our view of the process of Industrial Evolution, so far as it has progressed up to date. The condition is like that of an oak tree planted in a jar, or a chick developing within its shell; the indefinite continuance of the process is inconceivable. What form the collapse will assume, and when it may be expected to occur, is the problem next to be be taken up.

CHAPTER VI

THE REVOLUTION

ONE is at a great disadvantage just at present in picturing an industrial crisis. We are at the very flood-tide of prosperity; the railroads are paralysed by the volume of the country's business; the coal mines cannot furnish the coal, and the farmers are burning their grain because they cannot get it to market; the steel trust has orders for two years ahead—and so on without limit. I have to ask the reader to picture interest rates going down to zero, at a time when they are higher than they have been in a decade; I have to ask him to picture too much of everything in the country, at a time when there is not enough of anything. And yet all this excess of "prosperity" is an integral part of the phenomenon we are studying.

If the process of wealth concentration and overproduction of capital went on unmodified by any other factor, we should witness a gradual rise in the price of commodities, a gradual increase in the number of unemployed, and a gradual fall in the rates of interest. As it happens, however, the movement proceeds in rhythmic pulses, like the swinging of a pendulum, or the ebbing and flowing of the tide. This is owing to the factor of credit-expansion, which we have still to interpret.

We have pictured Capital, ubiquitous, endlessly resourceful, incessantly alert—"clamouring for dividends." Competition is a forcing-process by which every device that will increase profits is driven into general use, and subjected to its maximum strain. The most obvious of these devices is that of credit.

A business man has a certain amount of capital. If he makes his "turn over" once a year, he gains, say, ten per cent. profit; if he can make the "turn over" twice a year, he gains twenty per cent. He sees the business ahead, and so he goes into debt. And of course this step gives an impulse to the business of the man who manufactures his machinery, and to the man who raises his raw material, and to the railroads which handle both. The effect of that condition, prevailing throughout a whole community, is to accelerate enormously the industrial process; under it the capital of the community becomes, exactly as in the case of the railroads, not the actual definite cost of the instruments of production existing, but an altogether hypothetical thing, a function of anticipated earnings.

So it is that you have a "boom"—a period of furious and fevered activity, in which everyone sees fortunes springing up about him; and then comes some disturbing factor, which suggests to a number of men the advisability of realising on their expectations; and a chill settles upon the community, and there is a wild rush to collect, and the discovery is made that most of the anticipated profits are not in existence.

There is one more consideration which has to be touched upon before we are prepared to consider the concrete problem in America. The process which has been outlined is an industrial one; events have been pictured here as they would take place in a community given altogether to manufacturing, mining, and transportation. But as a matter of fact we have not only to reckon with thirteen billions a year of manufactured products, but also with four billions a year of farm products. The importance of this new element lies in the fact that the ownership of the farms is still largely in the hands of the masses; which means that once every year the process we have been picturing is stayed while the American people get rid of four billion dollars of spending money, which comes to them outside of and independent of the wage-fund. Thus, strange as it may seem, abundant crops tend to mitigate an "overproduction" crisis, while a failure of crops would do more than anything else in the world to precipitate one.

With these facts in mind we are now in position to interpret our recent industrial history. We have generally had our hard times in America at ten year intervals, with especially severe crises at twenty year intervals. We had our last severe attack in 1893, and we were due to have one of the lesser sort in 1903. What happened then was very interesting to watch, in the light of the views just explained. In the early winter and spring of 1904, the avalanche was well under way. Here, for instance, is an item clipped from the Chicago *Tribune* in April of that year:

"Organised labour is facing the greatest wage crisis since the panic of 1893, if the forecast of its leaders is correct. It is estimated that before the close of the year the greatest employing concerns of the country will have dismissed nearly one million men, most of them labourers and general-utility workers. Of this number the railroads are expected to discharge two hundred thousand employees; the mine operators, fifty thousand; the machine shops, iron, steel, and tin plate plants, two hundred and fifty thousand; and the building trades, forty thousand. The railroads and the

The Revolution 183

steel mills have already begun the work of reducing their forces, and the wage liquidation threatens to become as sensational as was the recent liquidation in stocks." And then on May 25th following, the New York *Herald* reported that the railroads of the country had laid off seventy-five thousand men; and quoted the following in an interview with James J. Hill:

"The whole question falls back primarily upon decreasing business and the reason for it. Why are the railroads carrying less freight than they were a year or two years ago? Because the demand for the products of the United States is not commensurate with the supply. We manufacture and we grow and we mine more than we can consume in the United States. Hence we are dependent upon foreign markets in order to sell the surplus."

The reasons why we got over this period of liquidation with only a severe scare are two: First, because there came in the fall a "bumper" crop of unprecedented proportions, which gave the railroads a new start; and second, and most important, because it happened that at the precise hour of our stress, there broke out one of the greatest military struggles of all history.

The war, you understand, was a new world-market. All at once a million or two of men were set to work at destroying manufactured articles; and at the same time several millions more were taken from their regular tasks to provide and maintain them while they did it; and the greater part of the surplus capital of civilisation was drawn off to pay the bills. It was not merely that during the first four months of the conflict Japan and Russia bought fifty million dollars' worth of our spare products, or that they took hundreds of millions of our spare cash. It made no real difference where the money was raised, or where it was spent; the man who got it spent it again, and sooner or later the bulk of it came to us, because we had the things to sell. Under the conditions of modern Capitalism, all the world is one; and when a nation goes to war, whoever has a spare dollar lends it to pay the bills, and wherever in the world there is an idle labourer, he is put to work to help support the fighters of both nations. In return, the world gets from the warring governments a paper promise to wring an equivalent amount of service out of their people at some future date.

Before going on I ought to mention that there is another view of the events of 1904. I have heard Mr. Arthur Brisbane maintain that we are to have no more overproduction crises, for the reason that, competition having been abolished in all our

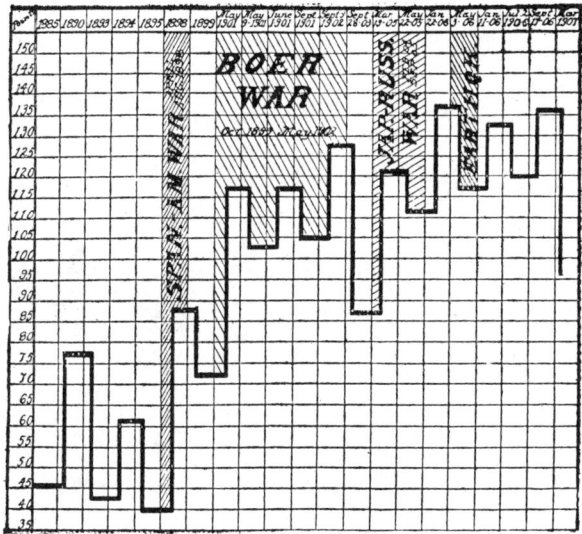

Diagram prepared by Wilshire's Magazine

DIAGRAM SHOWS HOW HIGH PRICES FOLLOW WARS
Range of average prices of 25 leading Railway Stocks for the past 22 years

The Revolution

principal industries, our trust magnates can so adjust supply to demand as to mitigate the stress, and give instead periods of partial idleness in widely scattered industries. If this is true, it is very important, for it means a long continuance of Trust government; but I do not believe that it is true. The trusts have, of course, put an end to blind production without any assurance of a market; but even assuming that our industry were so far systematised and our management so conservative that we never manufactured goods except upon a definite order—how would that be able to hold in check a community gone mad with prosperity-drunkenness? For instance, the steel trust now has orders enough ahead for two years; and upon the basis of these orders, its administrators are going ahead building a new "steel city." Yet does the steel trust know what proportion of its orders for steel rails are intended for the transportation of purely speculative freight? Does it know what proportion of its orders for structural steel is intended for buildings for imaginary tenants? Does it concern itself with the problem whether its customers are going to be able to find any use for the materials which they have bought?

There might be more plausibility in the argument, if our trust magnates were men of conscience and a keen sense of responsibility; but as a matter of fact their attitude toward their work is purely predatory. They are not administrators of production at all, but parasites upon production, exploiters and wreckers. Far from striving to regulate the madness of the public, they are competing among themselves to fan it to a flame, so that they may capitalise the expectations of their own properties.*

The ebb of the tide is coming; the only question is, when? According to precedent, it should come in 1913; but I expect it much sooner, partly because I do not believe that we had anything like a thorough liquidation in 1904, and partly because of the extreme violence of the present activity. During the last year the "boom" has reached real estate, and that always means that other avenues of investment are clogged.

I anticipate the storm in 1908 or 1909; but I do not predict it, because it depends upon uncertain factors. Another great war might put it off ten years; and on the other hand, crop failures might precipitate it this summer. What I do believe that I can predict—for reasons which I stated in the introduction to this argument—is the

---

*Anyone who wishes to make a scientific study of the true functions of modern finance is advised to read Professor Veblen's last book, "The Theory of Business Enterprise," a most extraordinary study of the whole field of present-day economics. In my opinion this book, together with its author's other masterpiece, "The Theory of the Leisure Class," constitutes the greatest contribution to social science ever made in America, and perhaps the greatest in the world since Carl Marx. It might be worth while to add in passing that Professor Veblen was turned out of Mr. Rockefeller's University of Chicago for writing it.

The Revolution

course which political events in this country will take from the hour when the "hard times" arrive.

As we saw from the Chicago *Tribune* item, the first sign of trouble is the turning out of work of a million workingmen; and what are the consequences—the economic consequences—of the turning out of work of a million men? According to the census the average yearly wage of the factory employee is four hundred and thirty-seven dollars. Dr. Peter Roberts says that the average wage in the anthracite coal district is less than five hundred dollars. In the Middle States a third of all the workers get less than three hundred a year, and in the South nearly sixty per cent. get less. It was proven before the Industrial Commission that the maximum wage of the hundred and fifty thousand railroad and track hands and the two hundred thousand carmen and shopmen, was a hundred and fifty dollars in the South, and less than three hundred and seventy-five in the North. And this to feed and clothe a family, and provide against sickness, accident, and old age! The meaning of it is simply that when a million men are laid off, in a month or two they and their families are starving.

And that, you understand, means a loss of a *market*—of a market of five million people—a population equal to that of the Dominion of Canada. And of course, therefore, those whose work it has been to supply these people, will be out of work, and likewise those who supply the suppliers. And even this is by far the least of the consequences; for another part of our domestic market depends upon the fact that our workingmen too have been able to form trusts. And when this period of depression comes, their trusts will fall to pieces, and competition will begin again—a process which they will find all the brickbats and dynamite in the country cannot check. The employers will, of course, be straining every nerve to make ends meet; and so wages will go down, and when strikes are declared, the starving workingman will "scab" and the strikes will fail. We shall have riots, and perhaps gatling guns in our streets, but the wages will go down; and step by step as the wages go down, consumption goes down, with the loss of another Dominion of Canada. When the thing is once started, it will be an avalanche that no power upon earth can stop; and it will be the beginning of the Revolution.

The word has an ominous sound. The reader thinks of street battles and barricades. By a Revolution I mean the complete transfer of the economic and political power of the country from the hands of the

The Revolution 189

present exploiting class to the hands of the whole people; and in the accomplishment of this purpose the people will proceed, as in everything else they do, along the line of least resistance. It is very much less trouble to cast a ballot than it is to go out in the streets and shoot: and our people are used to the ballot method. However, the staid and respectable *Harper's Weekly*, which calls itself a "Journal of Civilisation," suggested in 1896 that if Mr. Bryan were elected, it might be necessary for the propertied classes to keep him out of office. If anything of that sort is attempted in this coming crisis, why then there will be violence—just as there will be in such countries as Germany and Russia, which have yet to learn to let the people have their own way. The worst feature of the situation with us is that we have gotten into the habit of letting our elections be carried by bribery; and that is likely to play us some ugly tricks in this new emergency.

The reader perhaps objects to my theory that this change must come with suddenness. It is such a tremendous change—and would it not be better if it were brought about little by little? Undoubtedly it would have been a great deal better; but the time to begin was ten or twenty years ago. Now the horse is stolen, and we are venting all our energies, and cannot even succeed in getting the stable-door locked afterward.

They are bringing it about gradually in Australia and New Zealand—the only countries in the world in which the people are effectually regulating the progress of the Juggernaut of Capitalism. That is because these countries are very young, with comparatively little capital, no slums, and an intelligent working-class. I have an idea—I do not know whether there is anything in it—that the extraordinary success of New Zealand may in part be due to the fact that it was a convict-settlement; the men whom capitalism makes into criminals being for the most part a very superior class of people, active, independent, and impatient of injustice. Transported to a new land, and given a fair chance, I should think that a burglar or a highwayman ought to make a very excellent Socialist.

You ask, perhaps, if the thing is not also being accomplished gradually in England and on the Continent; you point to "Municipal trading," to the London County Council, to the state-owned railroads and telephones of Germany, Switzerland, Sweden, etc. You have been accustomed to hear these things referred to as State Socialism, and you have accepted the statement—not understanding that the essence of Socialism is democracy, and that it is

The Revolution

fundamentally opposed to paternalism in every conceivable form. Municipal and State ownership is not State Socialism at all, but State Capitalism. Under it, the government buys certain franchises, pays for them with bonds, and then runs the roads to pay the bondholders. Undoubtedly it is a better system for the people than private Capitalism, for the reason that it fixes the exploiters' tax, instead of letting stock-watering go on indefinitely. But, unfortunately, economical administration by the State is possible at present only in such countries as have an aristocratic governing-class, jealous of the power of the capitalist. In this country the holders of the municipal bonds, who also own the street-car factories and the steel-mills and the coal-mines, would use the interest they got from the city to bribe the city's servants to pay exorbitant prices for all the street-cars and steel rails and coal and other supplies which the city would have to have in order to operate the roads. You have seen that perfectly illustrated in the case of our Post Office. For example, we pay the railroads in rent for our mail-cars twice as much per year as it costs to build the cars; and the cars are so flimsy that the insurance companies, which own a large share of the railroads and the cars, refuse to insure the lives of the mail-clerks who work in them!

However, the advisability of Municipal Ownership under present conditions is a purely academic question, for the reason that the capitalist will never give us a chance to try it. The capitalist is in possession, and he "stands pat." When you talk about "reform," he will make you as many fine speeches and deliver you as many moral discourses as you wish; but when it comes to giving up any dollars—he has spent all his lifetime learning to hold on to his dollars.

You are thinking, perhaps, of President Roosevelt, who is hailed as a successful reformer. In the first place, it is of importance to point out that President Roosevelt is a complete anomaly in our political life; he was probably the last Republican in the country who would have been selected to rule us. He made himself governor by a shrewd device called "the Rough Riders;" he was made President for the first time by the bullet of an assassin, and the second time by the death of Mark Hanna. By a series of such blind chances as these the people have been given a chance to vote for what they want, and they of course have seized the chance. But assuredly it was no part of the "System's" plan to ask them what they wanted, nor even to let them find out what they wanted themselves.

Under the peculiar circumstances, there

The Revolution 193

has been nothing for the "System" to do but make sure that the President accomplishes nothing; and that it has done as a matter of course. In saying this, let me remind the reader once more of my distinction between moral revolt and economic remedy. I have no wish to under-estimate the tremendous importance of President Roosevelt's services in awakening the people; but I say that so far as actual concrete accomplishment is concerned, he might just as well never have lifted a finger. In one case, that of the suit against the Paper Trust, he did effect a lowering of prices; but in that case he was simply a pawn in the struggle between two trusts—of which the Newspaper Trust proved to be the stronger. In no case where the people alone were concerned has he effected any economic change whatever. The Northern Securities decision was evaded by another device; the Beef Trust and the Standard Oil suits ended with nominal fines. Over the rate regulation question we had two years' agitation—and not one single rate has been lowered. In the struggle for life-insurance reform, to which the President gave all his moral support, a few grafting officials were hounded to death; but the real and vital evil, the exploitation of the surplus for purposes of stock-manipulation, was scarcely even touched upon. And then came the Chicago packing-house scandals—and I can speak with some knowledge of them. Sometimes, when I look back upon them, it seems like a dream—I can hardly believe that I ever played my part in that cosmic farce. Only think of it—we had the President and Congress and all the newspapers of the country discussing it—we had this entire nation of eighty million people literally thinking about nothing else for months—nay, more, we had the attention of the whole civilised world riveted upon those filthy meat-factories. We uncovered crimes for which the condemnation of every dollar's worth of property in Packingtown would have been a nominal punishment; and then we settled back with a sigh of contentment, because we had put a few more inspectors at work and forced the whitewashing of some slaughter-house walls. And we left the monster upas-tree of commercialism to flourish untouched—to go on year after year bearing its fruit of corruption and death!

There is nothing whatever to be got from the capitalist. I used to think that the same thing was true of the politician. In common with most Socialists, I thought that the Revolution would have to wait until the people had come to full consciousness of their purpose, and had elected a Socialist president and a Socialist congress. But at the time of the coal-strike, when Dave Hill came out for government ownership of the coal mines, I realised that the politician is the jackal and not the lion. Of course we have amateur politicians—capitalists who play at the game—and they will not give way; but the professional politican is not a rich man—the competition has been too keen. He has served the capitalist because it paid; and when the people get ready to have their way, it will pay to serve the people. This is really a very important matter, for our political machinery is complicated, and the people have got used to it. It would be a frightful waste of energy to create new machinery—in fact, I do not think that our Constitution could stand the strain.

We will now assume that the industrial crisis has come. What will be the political consequences? It takes two or three years for industrial conditions to get themselves translated into political acts in this country; it means an immense amount of agitating— tens of thousands of meetings have to be held and hundreds of thousands of speeches made; and then there is all the machinery of conventions and elections. The panic of 1893, for instance, resulted in the Bryan movement of 1896. That movement was a revolt of the debtor class; if it had succeeded it would have precipitated a panic, and that would have been a misfortune, for the reason that both the people and their leaders were ignorant, and instead of the Industrial Republic, we should have had a severe reaction. Mark Hanna was a cunning man; but if he had been still more cunning, he would never have raised six million dollars to buy the presidency for William McKinley—he would have let the people have free silver, and then he would have had the people.

We came to the election of 1900 on the crest of a prosperity wave; but prosperity too takes its time to be realised, and so Hanna took the precaution to raise four million dollars and buy the election again.* And then came 1904, which, I think, was the most interesting election of them all. With the politicians the prosperity boom still held sway. Mark Hanna had Roosevelt all ready for the shelf; and the old-time "state-rights" Democrats arose and buried Mr. Bryan in the deepest vault of their party catacombs. But then came the people—with the country trembling on the verge of another "hard times." They gave President Roosevelt the most tremendous majority ever recorded in America; and incidentally, as if this were not enough to show how they felt, they gave

*Figures quoted, evidently upon inside information, by the Washington *Post*, in 1906.

The Revolution 197

nearly half a million votes to Eugene V. Debs!

This election, according to my schedule, corresponds with the election of 1852 in the Civil War crisis. The "safe and sane" Democracy, which received its death-blow in 1904, corresponds with the old Whig party. It will probably make independent nominations in 1908 and 1912, exactly as did the Whigs, and will receive the votes of all those who believe in dealing with new conditions according to old formulas.

In the meantime, the real contestants of the coming crisis are forming their lines. Under ordinary circumstances the Republican party would have been the party of disguised but unrelenting conservatism; and our Presidents in 1904 and 1908 would have been either figureheads like Fairbanks and Shaw, or shrewd beguilers of the people like Cannon and Root. As it is, it looks now if President Roosevelt were to remain the master of his party, in which case we shall have in 1908 a mild reformer like Taft, or possibly even Governor Hughes. The one thing certain is that whoever receives the Republican nomination will be the next President. If it is a Roosevelt man, the President's prestige will elect him; or if the "System" concludes to have its own way, he will be put in by bribery. In any case, he will go in, and it is best that he should go in. So long as we are to have Capitalism, it is proper that the capitalist should have a free hand. Personally I should consider the election of a radical in 1908 a calamity; for "hard times" will be just about to break, and I greatly desire to see Cannon and Aldrich and the rest of them "caught with the goods on."

Who will be the Democratic candidate? Will it be the champion of the Western farmers, or of the proletariat of our Eastern cities? I do not know, but I am inclined to think that it will be Mr. Bryan; and I am sorry, in a way, because that will put him out of the race in 1912. I conceived an intense admiration for Mr. Bryan after his last speech in New York City.

Never in our history did a public man face a greater temptation than he did after his two years of travel; everything in the country seemed to have turned conservative, and the money-power, frightened by Roosevelt, was ready to throw itself into his arms. What he did was to take his stand upon the great issue over which the battle of the next six years will be fought out—the nationalisation of the railroads; and in doing it he placed his name upon the roll of our statesmen.

A couple of years ago I was sketching out my comparison of the Civil War crisis and our own, in conversation with an English

The Type.	Chattel Slavery. (1846–1863.)	Wage Slavery (1893–1914.)
The Conservative Reformer	Daniel Webster.	Grover Cleveland.
The Unwilling Prophet	John C. Calhoun	Marcus A. Hanna.
The Great Compromiser	Henry Clay	Theodore Roosevelt.
The Timid Conservative	Edward Everett.	Alton B. Parker.
The Editor of Radicalism	Horace Greeley.	Arthur Brisbane
The Statesman of Radicalism	Charles Sumner.	Wm. J. Bryan.
The Politician of Radicalism	Wm. H. Seward.	Robt. M. LaFollette.
The Agitator of the Revolt	Wm. Lloyd Garrison.	Eugene V. Debs.
The Orator of the Revolt	Wendell Phillips.	Geo. D. Herron.
The Martyr of the Revolt	John Brown.	Charles H. Moyer (?).
The Voice of the Victim	Frederick Douglass.	Jack London.
The Compromising Reactionist	Stephen A. Douglas.	John C. Spooner.
The Aggressive Reactionist	Jefferson Davis.	Nelson W. Aldrich.
The Organiser of Reaction	Wm. Lownds Yancey.	David M. Parry.
The Last Figurehead	James Buchanan (1856).	William H. Taft (1908).
The Untried Hope	Abraham Lincoln (1860).	Wm. Randolph Hearst (1912).

gentleman, who asked me to make him a table showing the parallel between the men of the two periods. This table was afterwards published in the *Independent*, with an explanatory letter, (in the course of which I pointed out that one must not take it too literally, or look for a resemblance in external details).*

In the course of its editorial comment, the *Independent* suggested another parallel, that between "The Jungle" and "Uncle Tom's Cabin"; and then it went on to express its perplexity at my venturing to compare Hearst with Lincoln.

There is no man in our public life to-day who interests me so much as William Randolph Hearst. I have been watching him for ten years, during the last half-dozen of them weighing and testing him as the man of the coming hour. I do not say that he will be the man; all that I can say is that he stands the best chance of being the candidate of the Democratic party in 1912; and that the man who secures that nomination will, if he does his work (and for him to fail to do it is almost inconceivable) write his name in our history beside the names of Washington and Lincoln.

Mr. Hearst is one of the by-products of the industrial process—a member of the "second generation." You are to picture

---
*See table on page 199.

many thousands of young men, heirs of the enormous fortunes of our captains of industry; they are brought up in luxury, and in complete idleness—the world gives them *carte blanche*, with the result that at an early age they are sated with all the ordinary pleasures of human beings. And at the same time they have big, healthy bodies, and they crave excitement.

It would be interesting to compile a list of some of the things they have done. Of course, a great many simply follow in the footsteps of their fathers, and become commercial buccaneers; some devote themselves to automobiles and race-horses, some to society and gossip, some to mere brutal dissipation—such as the scions of the now extinct line of Pullman, who used to smash up the saloons of Chicago, and now and then amuse themselves by hurling brickbats through the windows of their father's home. Now and then there is one who goes in for big game, or for monkey-dinners, or for Sunday-schools, or for Socialism, or for flying-machines; and there was one who went in for newspapers!

His father was reluctant to humour the whim—he thought that a million-dollar racing-stable would cost less in the end than a forty-thousand dollar newspaper: which of course put the young man upon his mettle—made him set out to make the paper pay, and "show the old man." To make it pay he had to get circulation; and to get circulation he had to get something new—there was no use doing things like the old newspapers, which were not paying, but had to be funded by the political powers which used them. So once more you see capital, as I have pictured it—"like a wild beast in a cage, pacing about, watching for an opening here and there."

And where is the opening? Why, the people! The people, whom the merciless machinery of exploitation beats down and tramples upon, and pushes out of the way and forgets. They are brutalised and ignorant, they are stupid with toil—but yet they are human beings, they crave life. They never read newspapers—but give them what they want, and they will learn to read. Give them big head-lines, and a shock on every page; give them royalty and "high life," scandal and spice, battle, murder and sudden death—and then they will buy your paper.

It was good fun for Mr. Hearst to do this. Watching his newspapers, what has struck me most is the sheer audacity of them. Audacity is his characteristic quality, and it is a characteristic American quality—it places him among our national treasures, along with Mark Twain, and P. T. Barnum, and Buffalo Bill, and the Mississippi steamboats with the "nigger on the safety-valve."

The Revolution

I am told by friends of Mr. Hearst that his instinct from the start was for democracy. If so, so much the better; but it is not necessary to my hypothesis. A newspaper has to have editorial opinions; and they had best be opinions that please its readers. If we are to publish a paper for the masses to read, we must also voice the hopes and the longings of the masses.

So Mr. Hearst turned traitor to his class. He seems to have done this instinctively, and without pangs. I find, what is very singular and striking, that the members of his own class hate him, not only publicly, but personally. It seems to have pleased him to defy *all* their conventions. I was told, for example, that when he first came to New York, he made himself a scandal in the "Tenderloin." I was perplexed about that, for the members of our "second generation" are generally well known in the Tenderloin, and nobody calls it a scandal. But one young society man who had known Hearst well gave me the reason—and he spoke with real gravity: "It wasn't what he did—we all do it: but it was the way he did   He didn't take the trouble to hide what he did."

I have made clear in this book my belief that the masses are driven to revolt by the pressure of stern and ruthless economic force. They were ignorant and helpless, and among our men of wealth and power there was no one to help them—there was no one among all our intellectual leaders to voice their wrongs. They were left to help themselves—so what more natural than that it should occur to some enterprising young millionaire to leap into the breach? There was endless excitement and notoriety to be won—and at the end, perhaps, power of a new and quite incredible sort.

You will observe that I am taking, deliberately, the lowest possible view. I am dealing with material conditions and picturing a material remedy for them. My point is, that whatever he may be personally, Mr. Hearst is mortgaged, body and soul, to the course to which he has given himself; not only his public reputation, but his entire fortune, is in his newspapers, and the public is the master of his newspapers. He has conjured a storm which he cannot possibly control—he must play out to the end the part he has chosen.

It is very curious to observe how his rôle has taken hold of him and changed him. I am told that when he first came to New York he wore checked trousers and fancy ties; and now he wears the traditional soft hat and frock coat of our statesmen. And also, I think, the rôle has changed his character. For this struggle is a real one, it is

The Revolution

a struggle of the people for life; the cause is a cause of truth and justice, and the man does not live who can do battle for it as Mr. Hearst has done, and not come to take fire with the passion of it. The man does not live who can make the enemies Mr. Hearst has made, and not take a real and vital interest in the task of bringing them to their knees. I believe that Mr. Hearst is to-day as sincere a man as we have in political life.

It may be, of course, that some one else will get the Democratic nomination in 1912; that matters not at all in my thesis—the one thing certain is that it will be some man who stands pledged to put an end to class-government. Following it there will be a campaign of an intensity of fury such as this country has never before witnessed in its history.

Let us outline in a few words the situation as it will then exist.

In the first place there will be two or three million—perhaps five or ten million—men out of work. They will have been out for a year or two, and have had plenty of time to work up excitement. They may have forced Congress to provide them some temporary employment—which will, of course, be the first taste of blood to the tiger. They will certainly have been waging strikes of a violence never before known

—they will have been shot down in great numbers, and they may have done a great deal of burning and dynamiting. That some particularly conspicuous individual like Mr. Rockefeller or Mr. Baer may have been assassinated, seems more than likely; that a "Coxey's Army" of much larger size will have marched on Washington, seems quite certain.

When I was in Chicago, just after the last "Beef Strike," I met half a dozen labour leaders who told me an interesting story. Chicago has the most thoroughly revolutionary working class of any city in the country, and towards the end of this strike they were deeply stirred, and there had been several conferences in which a complete program had been laid out for an "anti-rent strike." On a certain day, all the working people of Chicago were to refuse to pay rent until the meat-packers gave in. The project was nipped by the settlement of the strike, but it only waits a new occasion to be put into effect. By the time which we are picturing here, it will quite certainly have spread east and west to the two oceans, so that not half our city population will be paying any rent for their homes at this time.

And also, of course, there will have been processions in the streets, and unemployed demonstrations every day. There will be a Socialist meeting round every corner—

Copyright, 1894, Leslie's Weekly

Copyright 1894, Leslie's Weekly

COXEY'S ARMY ON THE MARCH AND IN WASHINGTON

The Revolution

all through this period of stress, you are to picture the Socialists working like bees at swarming time. That is the function of the Socialist party all through this crisis, to stir up and organise the proletariat, to make certain that in the crisis the people are not ignorant of the way. They will be heading the hunger-parades, carrying the banners and making the speeches, circulating tracts and five-million-copy editions of the "Appeal to Reason." They will be polling unheard of votes—in one or two cities they will be carrying the elections, and Socialist mayors will be confiscating street-railroads, and clapping obstructive judges into jail. The Socialist party is a party of agitation rather than administration; but it is of vital importance that it should everywhere exist, as a party of the last resort, a club held over Society. Everywhere the cry will be: Do this, and do that, or the Socialists will carry the country.

So will be ushered in the election campaign and the death-grapple. You will try to beat the people back, as you have done before—but you will not succeed this time. Before this, the people were ignorant—but now they will know. They will have had the whole of the festering ulcer of commercialism laid open before their eyes. You will not be able to blame it on the labour unions, nor on the Rate Bill, nor on Roosevelt, nor on the Negro, nor on the Esquimau. You will not be able to awe the people with any great names, nor to fool them with respectability. They will have been taught to regard the leaders of our business affairs as convicted and unpunished criminals; and if you were to propose such a thing as a "business man's parade," you would be greeted with a scream of fury.

You will be utterly terrified at the state of affairs. Credit will be failing, and the business of the country will be holding its breath. You will subscribe a campaign fund of ten—fifteen—twenty millions of dollars—but there will be Mr. Hearst with his extras in a dozen cities, and his twenty million free copies a day, and he will tell how much you are raising and a whole lot more. So there will be committees of safety to guard the ballot—and a few more good campaign cries. There will be frenzied conferences among our political millionaires, and a week or two before election day Mr. Hearst's opponent—quite probably ex-President Roosevelt—will come out favouring nearly all of his radical proposals, but declaring that they ought not to be carried into effect by a Socialist like Mr. Hearst. Mr. Hearst will reply with his ten thousand and tenth declaration that he is

The Revolution 209

not a Socialist, and has no sympathy with Socialism—a statement which the Socialists, who will not understand in the least the meaning of events, will cordially substantiate. Mr. Hearst will declare that he stands upon a platform of Americanism, and that he seeks only equal rights for all—and therefore Federal ownership of all criminal monopolies.

So election day will come, and Mr. Hearst will be elected; and within the next week the business of the country will have fallen into heaps. Banks will have closed, mills will be idle—there will be no freight, and railroads will be failing. The people of New York will be reminded that if the railroads stop the city will starve to death in a couple of weeks; and so, perhaps even before Mr. Hearst takes office, government ownership of the railroads will be realised.

How will it be accomplished? It is a charmingly simple process—I could do it all myself. Have you ever heard the inside story of how the last coal strike was settled? The operators were standing upon their rights as the persons to whom God in His infinite wisdom had entrusted the care of the property interests of the country; and all winter long the people had been lacking coal. Then suddenly President Roosevelt, who is a master of the art of feeling the public pulse, made the discovery that government ownership of coal mines was about to crystallise into an issue of practical politics. So he sent Secretary Root to see Morgan, and tell him that the coal operators must give in. Morgan saw the operators, and they insisted upon their rights, and so Root went back to Washington, and came again to say that, as Mr. Morgan well knew, the coal roads were doing business in flat violation of the law; and that unless within twenty-four hours they gave their consent to the appointment by the President of a board of arbitration, the whole power of the United States Attorney General's office would be turned upon an investigation of their business methods. And so the strike was settled in a day.

And in very similar ways will the future problems be settled. There will be similar conferences; and then some fine day a duly-accredited commissioner from the President will travel, say to Philadelphia, and enter the offices of the Pennsylvania Railroad, arch-corrupter of the great Keystone state. The directors of the company will receive him with bows and smiles, and will spread their books before him and his staff, and place themselves and their office at his disposal. He will hear a brief account of the situation, and will then give his orders to the president and other officials of the

The Revolution

road: to the effect that schedules are to be continued as previously; that all salaries will remain unaltered until further notice; and that passenger and freight rates are to be dropped to a point where net profits will be wiped out. Then he will shake hands with the directors and thank them for their services in building up the road, adding that their services are now at an end. And that, for all practical purposes, will be the application of Socialism to the Pennsylvania Railroad.

But, you say, by my hypothesis the road could not run; how will it be able to run now? The reason it couldn't run before was that there were no profits; but now it will not be run for profits, but for service, like the Post Office. To help it over its momentary embarrassment, of course, the credit of the government may be needed: but even that is not likely. For exactly the same thing which happens to the Pennsylvania Railroad will be happening to the Steel Trust and the Oil Trust and the Coal Trust and the Beef Trust; and all these industries will be starting into activity, and so there will be plenty of freight. With the captains of each of these trusts there will have been secret Presidential conferences, at which these gentlemen will have been told that since they can no longer run their business, they must allow the

Government to take possession and run it—the price to be paid for their stock being a matter for future negotiation, and a matter of no great importance to them in any case, because of the income and inheritance tax laws just then being rushed through Congress.

Such will be the Revolution—and the gateway into the Industrial Republic. Precisely as in France we saw that the peasant who was starving because he could not pay his taxes, began to till the land and grow rich without any taxes, so in the midst of universal destitution, it will suddenly be discovered that the farmer who could not sell his grain, and therefore had no hat to wear, may now exchange his grain with the operative in the hat factory who had produced so many hats for his master that he was himself out of a job, and could not get any bread. And all the cotton mills which were shut because we could no longer sell shirts to the Chinamen, will now start merrily to work making shirts for all the shirtless wretches the length and breadth of America. And the shoe operatives of Massachusetts, who were making shoes for the Filipinos, which the poor Filipinos had to be forced at the point of the bayonet to buy, will begin making shoes for their own children, and for the unhappy people of the tenements who were before going barefooted. And the Steel Trust will suddenly leap into action, because those misery-smitten four hundred thousand families in the "dark rooms" of the New York City tenements will now earn money to build themselves decent habitations. And the tens of thousands of little boys and girls who are now being ground up in the glass-factories of New Jersey and the cotton-mills of Georgia and the coal-mines of Pennsylvania, will come out into the sunlight and play, while their parents are building schools to which they can be sent. And the young girl who stands shuddering on the brink of prostitution, working ten hours a day in an East Side sweat-shop for a wage of forty cents a week, will receive the full value of her product, and be able to maintain herself by two hours of work a day.

I know what is the attitude of the medical profession towards a "cure-all"; and yet it is but the sober truth that for nearly every evil that troubles our age there is one remedy and only one—the democratisation of our industry. If you were to take a growing boy and rivet an iron band about his chest, there would come sooner or later a time when the boy would show symptoms of distress—and for every symptom there would be but one remedy. Is the boy cross and complaining? Break the band!

Is he pale and sickly? Break the band! Does he gasp and cry out? Break the band! Do you not know that in the monarchy of France, in the year 1780, a man who set out to find a remedy for this or that evil of the hour would have found but one remedy for all of them—the overthrowing of the aristocracy? And similarly all the diseases of this period, which are the despair of the moralist and the patriot, are consequences of the fact that our society is gasping in a last desperate agony of effort to maintain its system of competitive industry. We are like a man running on a railroad track pursued by a train. The train is increasing its speed, and do what he will, it gains upon him; he cries out, he gasps for breath, he is agonised, wild with terror, making his last leap with the engine at his very heels—and then suddenly it occurs to him to leap to one side, and so the train flashes by, and he sits down and mops his brow and thinks how very stupid it was of him!

CHAPTER VII

THE INDUSTRIAL REPUBLIC

AND now let us imagine that society has abolished exploitation and the competitive wage-system, and got its breath and found leisure to examine itself under the new régime. How will it find things proceeding?

One of the first objections that you will run up against, if ever you start out to agitate Socialism, is your lack of definiteness. Give us your program, people will say—we want to know what sort of a world you expect to make, and how you are going to make it. And they will grow angry when they find that you have not a cut-and-dried scheme of society in your pocket—that you have stirred them up all to no purpose. And yet that is just what you have to go on doing. There used to be Utopian Socialists—Plato was the first of them and Bellamy was the last—who knew the coming world from its presidents to its chimney-sweeps; who could tell you the very colour of its postage-stamps. But nowadays all Socialists are scientific. They say that social changes are the product of the interaction of innumerable forces, and cannot be definitely foretold; they say that the new organism will be the result of the strivings of millions of men, acted upon by various motives, ideals, prejudices and fears. And so they call themselves no longer builders of systems, but preachers of righteousness; their answer to objectors is that I once heard given by Hanford, recent candidate for vice-president on the Socialist ticket, to a lawyer with whom he was debating: "Do you ask for a map of Heaven before you join the Church?"

This much we may say, however. The Industrial Republic will be an industrial government of the people, by the people, for the people. Exactly as political sovereignty is the property of the community, so will it be with industrial sovereignty—that is, capital. It will be administered by elected officials and its equal benefits will be the elemental right of every citizen. The officials may be our presidents and governors and legislatures, or they may be an entirely separate governing body, corresponding to our present directors and presidents of corporations. In countries where the revolution is one of violence they will probably be trade-union committees. The governing power may be chosen separately in each trade and industry, by those who work in it, just as the officials of

The Industrial Republic

a party are now chosen by those who vote in it; or they may be appointed, as our postmasters and colonial governors are appointed, by some central authority, perhaps by the President. All of these things are for the collective wisdom of the country to decide when the time comes; meanwhile it is only safe to say that there will be as little change as possible in the business methods of the country—and so little that the man who should come back and look at it from the outside, would not even know that any change had taken place. I have heard a distinguished Republican orator, poking fun at Socialism in a public address, picture women disputing in the public warehouses as to whether each had had her fair share of shoes and fish. In the Industrial Republic the workingman will go to the factory, will work under the direction of his superior officer, and will receive his wages at the end of the week in exactly the same way as to-day. He will spend his money exactly as he spends it to-day—he will go to a store, and if he gets a pair of shoes he will pay for them. The farmer will till his land exactly as he does to-day, and when he takes his grain to market he will be paid for it in money, and will put it in the bank and will draw a check upon it to pay for the suit of clothes he has ordered by express. The only difference in all these various operations will be that the factories will be public property, and the wages the full value of the product, with no deductions for dividends on stock; and that the street cars, the banks and the stores will be public utilities, managed exactly as our post-office is managed, charging what the service costs, and making no profits. In the year 1901 the U. S. Steel Corporation paid one hundred and twenty-five million dollars and employed one hundred and twenty-five thousand men; under Socialism the wages of each employee of the U. S. Steel Corporation would therefore be increased one thousand dollars a year, which is two or three hundred per cent. In the same way, the wages of an employee of the Standard Oil Company would be increased four thousand dollars, which is from eight to ten hundred per cent. The fare upon the government-owned street railroads in the City of Berlin is two and a half cents, which would mean that our workingman's car-fare bill would be cut by fifty per cent. The toll of the government-owned telephone of Sweden is three cents, which would mean that the workingman's telephone bill would be cut seventy per cent. The elimination of the speculator and the higher piracy of Wall Street would raise the price of the farmer's grain by fifty per cent.; the elimination of the millers' trust and the railroad

The Industrial Republic

trust would lower the price of bread by an equal sum. The elimination of the tariff on wool, of the sweater and the jobber, the department store and the express trust, would probably lower the price of the farmer's suit of clothes sixty per cent; the elimination of the sweatshop and the slum might raise it to its original level, while decreasing the farmer's doctor's bills correspondingly. Of course I do not mean to say that the gains from the abolition of exploitation will be distributed in exactly the ratios outlined above. They will be distributed so as to equalise the rewards of labour. The point is that there will be a saving at every point—because at every point there is exploitation.

I have sketched in "The Jungle" (Chapter 36) a few of the social savings incidental to the abolition of competition. The reader who cares for a thorough and scientific study of the subject is referred to a recently published book, "The Cost of Competition," by Sidney A. Reeve. I had never heard of Professor Reeve until his publishers sent me his book. They say that he worked on it for seven years; and when I read it I counted myself that many years to the good, for I had meant to try to do the task myself. Professor Reeve has done it in a way which leaves not a word to be said. It is a marvellous analysis of the whole of our present productive system; and best of all, it is free from the jargon of the schools—it is the work of a man who has kept in touch with actual life, and has moral feeling as well as scientific training.

Professor Reeve analyses, not merely the "economic costs" of competition, but also the "ethical costs," which after all are the most important. The difference to the workingman will be, not merely that his wages will be several times as great, but that he himself will no longer be a wage slave, obliged to serve another man for his bread, to cringe and grovel for a a job, to toil all day for another man's profit, and save up his little hoard and live in dread of the next wage reduction, the next strike, or the next closing down of the factory. He will be a free and independent member of a coöperative State. He will be delivered from the necessity of getting the better of his neighbour, because his neighbour will no longer be able to get the better of him. He will be certain of permanent employment, without possibility of loss or failure of payment—certain that so long as he works he will receive just what he produces, that in case of accident or old age he will be maintained, and that in case of death his children will be cared for and brought up to become coöperative partners in the great Industrial Republic.

From "The Cost of Competition"
THE COOPERATIVE DISTRIBUTION OF INFORMATION
The Congressional Library

From "The Cost of Competition"
THE COMPETITIVE DISTRIBUTION OF INFORMATION

The Industrial Republic

How, you ask, could Socialism guarantee every man permanent employment? Could there not be overproduction under Socialism? There could not; the surplus product being the property of the man who had produced it, and not, as now, the property of some other man, in a case of overproduction the workingman would be, not out of work, but on a vacation. As a matter of fact, only a reasonable surplus would be produced, because the workingman would stop when he had produced what he wanted— just as you stop eating when you have satisfied your hunger.

In the Industrial Republic there will be an administrative officer, a cabinet official with a bureau of clerks, whose task it will be to register the decrees of the law of supply and demand. It is found, let us assume, that the amount of coal needed by the community is represented by the labour of two million men, five days in the week, and six hours a day; the number of shoes is represented by the labour of half a million men the same time. The wages in each trade are ten dollars a day, and at this rate it is found that two million men go to the shoe factories to work and only half a million to the coal mines. The wages of coal mining are therefore made twelve dollars, and the wages of shoe-making eight dollars; if the balance still does not adjust itself, it will at the rate of thirteen to seven, or fourteen to six. Every week the government list shows the wages that can be earned in the various trades; stoking in a steamship is a painful and dangerous task—stokers in steamships are receiving twenty dollars a day, and still few takers, so that the steamships have to be fitted with stoking machinery at once. On the other hand, driving a rural-delivery mail-wagon is pleasant work, and is paying at present only five dollars a day, and with prospects of going still lower. And does all this seem fantastic to you? But it is exactly the way our employment problem is solved to-day, when it is solved at all; it is solved by means of "Help Wanted" advertisements and *viva voce* rumours—imperfectly, blindly and sluggishly, instead of instantly, intelligently and consciously by a universal government information bureau. Out in the country where I lived two years ago the farmers were unable to get help for love or money, while millions were out of work and starving in the cities; and that is only one of the thousands of illustrations one could give of "how much depends, when two men go out to catch a horse, upon whether they devote their time to catching him, or to preventing each other from catching him."

The *Independent* recently published an article entitled "Poverty: Its Cause and

Cure," by Mr. James Mackaye, a Harvard graduate and technological chemist; in the course of its editorial comment the paper hailed his plan for the abolition of poverty as "nothing less than a very great invention." "It adds something that was lacking in the older schemes of Socialism," the *Independent* continued, "but absolutely necessary to any Socialism that would be practically workable." This "something" is a device to increase the salaries of managers of the various industrial departments in proportion as they reduced the "producing time" of the commodity for which they were responsible. Mr. Mackaye is another student who, like Professor Reeve and Professor Veblen, have come into Socialism by their own routes. In his elaborate book, "The Economy of Happiness," he shows so thorough a grasp of the whole subject that I cannot suppose him to share in the ignorance of the literature of modern proletarian Socialism, which leads the *Independent* to hail his plan as a "great invention." As a matter of fact, I could name a score of Socialist books and pamphlets in which such plans are suggested and discussed. I personally have always rejected them as unsound in theory and unnecessary in practice. I have already suggested the likelihood of a continuance of present official salaries after the revolution; but there will be a strong tendency to reduce these, and I can see no ultimate result except equality of compensation by the State. I can see no theoretical basis for the State's paying to any employee more than it pays to another in the same industry—hand-labour being equally as necessary to the production of wealth as is superintendence. To my mind, the only necessary stimulus to efficiency is the community of interest of all the workers. The incentive to the manager is emulation, and the higher range of activity which goes with a position of command; and I should be very jealous of the introduction of any pecuniary motive into the struggle for promotion—as likely to continue the old evils of graft and favouritism to which we are now subject. I do not think that, when you have so organised industry that every man is working for himself, you will find it necessary to employ any outside force to impel him to work; and in fact I should consider it a violation of the rights of the worker to attempt anything of the sort. Of course if the workers themselves chose to offer a bonus to a manager to invent new methods, that would be another matter; but that would come under the head of intellectual production, which I shall consider later on.

In discussing the question of salaries,

it is to be pointed out what a vast difference will be made in the amount of money which every individual needs, by the socialisation of all the leading industries. In the Industrial Republic a thousand dollars a year will buy more comfort and happiness than ten thousand in the world as at present organised. There will come, at the very outset, the great economic savings already outlined; and then, the whole power of the coöperative mind of man being applied to the elimination of waste and the making of beauty and joy, we shall have in a very short time a world in which few men will care to cumber themselves with possessions of any sort excepting the clothes upon their backs and the few tools of their intellectual trades,—books, music, etc. The abolition of privilege and class-exploitation will of course wipe out at a stroke all that competition in ostentation which Professor Veblen has entititled "conspicuous consumption of goods." In the Industrial Republic there will be no luxury, for there will be no slavery. There will be no menial service of any sort under Socialism. I believe that this gives one a key by which he can do a great deal of predicting as to what will be found in the world when the impending revolution has taken place. In the Industrial Republic no man will work for another man—except for love—because no other man will be able to pay the "prevailing rate of wages."

It is the vision of this that makes the critics of Socialism cry out that it will destroy the home. What they mean is that it will destroy that kind of a home which exists upon a basis of butlers, cooks and kitchen maids, banquets and carriages, jewellery and fine raiment, sweat shops, and slums, prostitution, child-labour, war and crime. Unless I am very much mistaken, those people who now wear diamonds, and decorate their homes with all sorts of objects of "art," would do a great deal less of it if they had to pay for it with their own toil—if they were not able to pay for it with money extracted from the toil of others. I imagine that those who now, in our restaurants and banquet halls, gorge themselves upon the contents of earth, sea, and sky, would dine very much more simply—and very much more wholesomely—if they had to wash the dishes. For this reason, I expect that in the Industrial Republic there will be very little of that pseudo-art which ministers to vanity and sensuality. Our houses and clothing will become simpler and more dignified, and the artist will turn his thoughts to public works—he will decorate the parks and public buildings, the theatres, concert halls and libraries, the great coöperative dining halls and apartment houses. In the cities and towns of the Industrial Republic there will of course be possibilities of beauty such as we cannot even dream of at present. Now our cities grow haphazard, and are typical of all our blindness, selfishness, and misery. At every turn in them one comes upon new and more painful signs of these things— filthy and horrible slums, blatant and vulgar advertisements, insolent rich people in carriages, wan and starving children in the gutters. In the Industrial Republic a city will be one thing, and a work of art. It will not be crowded, for the combination of poverty and the railroad trust will not make spreading out impossible. Intelligent, coöperative effort having become the rule, nearly all the things that are now done privately and selfishly will be done socially. Manual work will not be a disgrace, and poverty will not keep any man ignorant, filthy and repulsive. There will be no classes and no class-feeling. There will be not only public schools and academies— there will be public playgrounds for all children, and clubs and places of recreation for men and women. In the Industrial Republic you will not mind going to such places and letting your children go. You will not be afraid of disease, because there will be public hospitals for all the sick; and you will not be afraid of rowdies, because the rowdy is a product of the slum, and there will not be any slum.

At present, we are all engaged in a struggle to beguile as much money out of each other as we can; and the State has nothing to do save to stand by and see fair play—and commonly finds that task too much for it! As a consequence, we find ourselves confronted with an infinite variety of little petty exactions—we have to spend money every time we turn around. Very soon after the Revolution, I fancy, men will begin to realise that these little exactions are more of a nuisance than a saving. For instance, I shall be very much surprised, if, a generation from now, the use of postage-stamps is not abolished. At present, with society wasting so immense a portion of its energy in competitive advertising, every piece of matter which goes into the mail has to be made to pay its way; but once do away with competition, and the only mail is government documents and personal letters—and the time it takes to stamp and cancel them will be many times greater than the cost of carrying the additional number of letters that a free mail service would bring forth. In the same way it will be found not worth while to employ conductors and spotters, and print tickets and transfers; after that we shall ride free on our street-cars, and perhaps ultimately in our government railroad trains. Similarly, all our places of recreation and of artistic expression would come to be free; and then some one would realise the waste incidental to our present system of book buying, and we should then have a universal national library, from which at frequent intervals delivery service would bring you any books then in existence. I have just witnessed in New York an exhibition of an invention which will make music as free as air. Bellamy was ridiculed for predicting "electric music" in the year 2000; and it is on sale in New York City in the year 1907. By this marvellous machine, the "telharmonium," all previously existing musical instruments are relegated to the junk heap; and all music composed for them becomes out of date. At one leap the art of music is set free from all physical limitations, and the musician is given command of all possible tones, and may play to ten thousand audiences at once. It is worth while pointing out, that, living under the capitalist system as we are, the inventor had no recourse save to use his machine to make profits, and so the newspapers, which are also in business for profits, left it to make its own way. So it came about that the first public exhibition of an invention which means more to humanity than any discovery since the art of printing, received mention in only one New York paper, and that to the extent of three or four inches.

But to return to the Revolution, and the first steps which have to be taken.

There are some industries which anyone can see are all ready for public ownership; and when the people have once found out the way, they will be very impatient with all remaining forms of rent, interest, profit and dividends. Also, the exploiters will soon learn to give way. Just as soon as the proprietors of department stores find that the people seriously intend to open a public store in every city, and to sell goods at cost, they will be glad to sell out for a few cents on the dollar; just as soon as the bankers find out that there is really to be a national bank, charging no interest, and incapable of failing, they will do the same with their buildings and outfits. To quote a paragraph from "The Jungle" (page 405), "The coöperative Commonwealth is a universal automatic insurance company and savings bank for all its members. Capital being the property of all, injury to it is shared by all and made up by all. The bank is the universal government credit account, the ledger in which every individual's earnings and spendings are balanced. There is also a universal government bulletin, in which are listed and precisely described everything which the Commonwealth has for sale. As no one makes any profit by the sale, there is no longer any stimulus to extravagance, and no misrepresentation, no cheating, no adulteration or imitation, no bribery, no 'grafting.'"

There remains only one other great problem to be mentioned—that of agriculture. I think no one will want to interfere with the farmer, any more than with the cobbler, the small storekeeper, the newsman or any other petty business. The farmer will stay on his land, and make money—and study the situation. He will find in the first place that coöperation is a success, and has come to stay. He will find that while he is working with his hands, the rest of society is working with steam and electricity, and leaving him far behind. He will find that he can no longer hire help—that his hired man is employed as a coöperative worker, and receiving several times more than the farmer himself. He will understand that to get his share of all the good things of the new civilisation, he will have to put his land into the common fund, and work for the commonwealth and not for his own wealth. In this case, of course, all the risks and losses of his trade will be shared by the whole community—the result of a bad crop in Maine being made up by a good crop in California, so that the farmer who works will be as certain of gain and as free from care as the factory hand.

And now let us consider the effect of this new system upon certain of the leading features of our civilisation. What, for instance, will be the effect of Socialism upon crime? The man who becomes a criminal at present finds himself in a world where he is compelled to work for some other man's profit, and to have flaunted in his face every hour the wealth which has been exacted from his toil. But now he will find himself in a world from which luxury and pauperism have been banished, and in which coöperation and mutual fellowship is the law. He will find that he gets just what he produces, and that he can produce in a day more than he can steal in a month. Don't you think that the criminal may find these powerful motives to become a worker? He may be a degenerate, of course, in which case we shall put him in a hospital; we should do that now, if we did not feel dimly that it would be of no use, because our social system is making criminals faster than we can pen them up, and makes the life of the majority of the working class so horrible that men have been known to steal on purpose to get into jail.

I have tried in "The Jungle" to give a picture of the process whereby the forces of commercialism turn honest workingmen into criminals and tramps. There is also another story to which I would refer the reader who cares to have more acquaintance with such conditions—"An Eye for an Eye," by Clarence Darrow.—And also, while we are considering this subject, let us not forget how the change would affect the criminals of the future, the wretched children of the slums and gutters, who will now be cared for by the State, and made into decent citizens in public asylums and hospitals, training schools and playgrounds.

What will be the effect of Socialism upon prostitution? Any young girl can go to the public factories or stores, to the coöperative boarding houses and hotels, the schools and nursery playgrounds, and secure employment for the asking, and support herself by a couple of hours' work a day in decent and attractive surroundings. She will, moreover, be able to marry the man who loves her, because the problem of a living will no longer enter into the question of marriage. She will be able to restrict her family to as many as she and her husband care to support, because she will be as intelligent and sensible as the women of our present upper classes.

The question of the relationship of the system of wage-slavery to the lives of women is too vast a one to be even outlined here; suffice it to say that the Socialist battle is the battle of woman, even more than it is the battle of the workingman. I cannot do better than to refer the reader to another book in which the whole question of the effects which age-long conditions of economic inferiority has wrought in the minds and bodies of women is discussed in scientific and yet fascinating form—Mrs. Gilman's "Woman and Economics."

What will be the effect of Socialism upon drunkenness? Under Socialism the workingman will have a decent home, and attractive clubs, reading rooms, and places of entertainment of all sorts, with plenty of time to frequent them. He will have steady employment, wholesome food, a pleasant place to work in, and—railroad fares being almost nothing—a trip to the country when he fancies it. His wife will not be an overworked, repulsive drudge, and his children will not be starving brats. When he wants a drink he will go to a public drinking-place and get it; what he gets will be pure, and will be sold him by a man who has no interest in getting him drunk. On the contrary, the attendant may be getting a royalty upon all non-intoxicating drinks he sells, and the drinker will quite certainly be paying a big tax upon all the intoxicating drinks he buys. Do you not think that all this may have some effect upon the nation's drink bill, which now is doubling itself every decade?

Recently I was invited by the *Christian Herald* to contribute to a symposium upon the question of prohibition. I wrote as follows: "In my opinion the drink evil is primarily an effect, and not a cause; it is a by-product of wage slavery. The working classes are to-day organised as the bond slaves of capital. The conditions under which they live are such as to brutalise and degrade them and drive them to drink. As I have phrased it in "The Jungle," if a man has to live in hell, he would a great deal rather be drunk than sober. The solution of the drink evil waits upon the coming of Socialism.

"As a part of the capitalist system, you have liquor sold for profit, and the liquor interests are one of the forces which dominate the land. Therefore, you are unable to effect any legislation to correct the evil. Liquor is sold in order to make money out of the victim, therefore every inducement and temptation is laid before him. Under Socialism, the only barkeeper would be the community, and the community would have every object in limiting the traffic. The children of the masses would be taken in hand and taught the secret of right living; and when they grew up they would have enough to eat and the means of keeping in working condition, and would know other sources of happiness than drunkenness. At present, attempts to reform the evil are attempts to sweep back the tide. Moreover, it is to be noticed that many of those who are most active in the work are themselves busily engaged in exploiting the working class in their private business, and are therefore directly identified with the cause of the evil they are attempting to combat."

What will be the effect of Socialism upon war? The New York *Sun* recently expressed the opinion that the end of war will come only with the Golden Age. If so, the Golden Age is within sight of all of us. Socialism will abolish war as inevitably, as naturally and serenely, as the sunrise abolishes the night. The cause of war is foreign markets; and under Socialism the markets will all be at home. Under Socialism the existence of the workers of the United States, of England, Germany, and Japan, will not be dependent upon the ability of their masters to sell their surplus products for profit to Chinamen. Under Socialism an International Congress will take in hand the backward nations, will clean out their sewers and wipe out their plagues and famines, their kings and their capitalists, their ignorance, their superstition and their

wars. It will do these things because they
need to be done—it will not do them as a
mere pretence to cover greed for gold mines
and markets. Outside of mines and markets there is no longer any cause of war,
save the old race hatreds which these have
begotten; and race hatreds are not known
among Socialists. In their last International Congress a Russian and a Japanese
shook hands upon the platform, while their
countrymen were flying at each other's
throats in Manchuria. The Socialist movement is a world-movement—it has brought
under its banners, working shoulder to
shoulder, men and women of all religions,
races and colours. With their victory, and
only with their victory, will the efforts of
"Peace Congresses" bear fruit.

Finally, what will be the effect of Socialism
upon the "System"? It is important to
distinguish between corruption as a sporadic
event, an accident here and there, and
corruption as a national institution. In
the Industrial Republic a worker might of
course bribe his foreman to let him cheat
the community; but that would be every
man's loss, and there would be every inducement to find it out and make it known, and
no hindrance whatever to its punishment.
At present, however, we have corruption
organised in town, county, city, state, and
nation, with every inducement to keep it

hidden, and almost no possibility of punishing it. Everybody understands that we have corporations, and that the corporations rule us; all that everybody does not yet understand is that the continuance of their rule would mean the ruin of free institutions in America, and ultimately the downfall of civilisation itself.

I have outlined the economic and political conditions which I believe will prevail in the Industrial Republic; there remains to consider what influences these will exert upon the moral and intellectual life of men. When people criticise the Socialist programme they always think about government censors and red tape, and limitations upon free endeavour; and so they say that Socialism would lead to a reign of tameness and mediocrity. They tell us that under the new régime we should all have to wear the same kind of coat and eat the same kind of pie. They argue that if all the means of production are owned by the Government there will be no way for you to get your own kind of pie; failing to perceive that government control of the means of production no more implies government control of the product, than government control of the post-office means government control of the contents of your letters. Said a good clergyman friend of mine: "What possible place, for instance, would there be for *me* in your Socialist society." And I answered, "There would be just exactly the same place for you that there is at present. How is it that you get your living and your freedom? You are maintained by an association of people who want the work you can do. Every clergyman in the country is maintained in that way—and so are thousands upon thousands of editors, authors, artists, actors—so are all our clubs, societies, restaurants, theatres and orchestras. The Government has absolutely nothing to do with them at present—and the Government need have absolutely nothing to do with them under Socialism. The people who want them subscribe and pay for them. Under our present system they pay the cost to private profit-seekers; under Socialism they would pay the State."

In the Industrial Republic a man will be able to order anything he wishes, from a flying machine to a seven-legged spider made of diamonds; and the only question that anyone will ever dream of asking him will be: "Have you got the money to pay for it?" There remains only to add that, the system of wealth-distribution being now one of justice, that question will mean: "Have you performed for society the equivalent of the labour-time of the article you desire society to furnish you?"

Nine-tenths of the argument against Socialism dissolves into mist the moment one states that single all-important fact, that Socialism is a science of *economics*. For instance, Mr. Bryan has recently published in the *Century Magazine* an article entitled "Individualism versus Socialism;" and here is the way he contrasts the two: "The individualist believes that competition is not only a helpful but a necessary force in society, to be guarded and protected; the Socialist regards competition as a hurtful force, to be entirely exterminated." Now there are endless varieties of competition with which Socialism could in no conceivable way interfere: the competition of love, and of friendship; the competition of political life; the competition of ideals, of music and books, of philosophy and science. It is the claim of the Socialists that by setting men free from the money-greed and the money-terror—from the need of struggling to deprive other men of the necessities of life in order to prevent them from depriving you of these necessities—the mind of the race would be set free for more vigorous competition in these other fields, and thus the development of real individuality would be for the first time made possible. This being the desire of the Socialist, it should be clear how fundamental is the misconception of Mr. Bryan, indicated by the bare title of his article—"Individualism *versus* Socialism." Socialism is not opposed to Individualism, and to set the two in opposition is like the attempt to imagine a fight between an elephant and a whale.

Socialism is a proposition for an economic re-organisation; as such, the only thing to which it can logically and intelligently be opposed is Capitalism. Mr. Bryan indicates that he discerns this, in another portion of his article. He says; "For the purpose of this discussion Individualism will be defined as the private ownership of the means of production and distribution where competition is possible, leaving to public ownership those means of production and distribution in which competition is practically impossible; and Socialism will be defined as the collective ownership, through the State, of all the means of production and distribution." For general unfairness this statement makes me think of the story of a man who was riding through the country and stopped to admire a fine pair of turkeys, and after praising them with enthusiasm, remarked to the farmer: "I will match you for them! Heads they are mine, and tails they stay yours." Mr. Bryan has composed a subtly worded definition of Individualism which takes all the kernels from the Socialist ear, and leaves to the Socialist only the husk. "Leaving to public ownership those means of production and distribution in which competition is practically impossible!" What a beautiful field for controversy, and what endless opportunities for compromise and concession, for advance or retreat! Ten years ago Mr. Bryan would not have appreciated the necessity of inserting this clause; industrial evolution had not proceeded quite so far, and all our radicals were bending their efforts to destroying the trusts. It was only after the last presidential election, unless I am mistaken, that Mr. Bryan definitely committed himself to the public ownership "of those means of production and distribution in which competition is practically impossible."

If Mr. Bryan would only procure and read a really authoritative treatise upon modern scientific Socialism (say Vandervelde's "Collectivism and Industrial Evolution") he would understand that his programme is so close to that of the Socialists that the difference would require a microscope to discern. In fact, I imagine that the majority of modern proletarian thinkers would be willing to subscribe to the programme of "Individualism" exactly as Mr. Bryan states it: "the private ownership of the means of production and distribution where competition is possible, leaving to public ownership those means of production and

The Industrial Republic

distribution in which competition is practically impossible."

The one point to be made absolutely clear in this matter is that the Industrial Republic will be an organisation for the supplying of the *material necessities* of human life. With the moral and intellecual affairs of men it can have very little to do. What Socialism proposes to organise and systematise is industry, not thought. The difference between the products of industry and those of thought is a fundamental one. The former are strictly limited in quantity, and the latter are infinite. No man can have more than his fair share of the former without depriving his neighbour; but to a thought there is no such limit—a single poem or symphony may do for a million just as well as for one. With the former it is possible for one man to gain control and oppress others; but it is not possible to monopolise thought. And it is in consequence of this fact that laws and systems are necessary with the things of the body, which would be preposterous with the things of the mind. The bodily needs of men are pretty much all alike. Men need food, clothing, shelter, light, air, and heat; and they need these of pretty nearly the same quality and in pretty nearly the same quantity—so that they can be furnished methodically year in and year out, according to order. This is being done by our present industrial masters for profit; in the Industrial Republic it will be done by the State, for use.

Quite otherwise is it with things in which men are not alike—their religions and their arts and their sciences. The only conditions under which the State can with any justice or efficiency have to do with production in these fields, is after men have come to agreement—when opinion has given place to knowledge. For instance, we have, in certain fields of science, methods which we can consider as agreed upon; it would be perfectly possible for the State to endow astronomical investigators, and seekers of the North Pole, and inventors of flying machines, and pioneers in all the technical arts. In the same way we come to agree, within certain limits, what is a worth-while play or book; in so far as we agree, we can have government theatres and publishing houses, government newspapers and magazines. If ever science should discover the rationale of the phenomenon of genius, so that we could analyse and judge it with precision, we should then have the whole problem solved.

You are a writer, perhaps; and you say that you would not relish the idea of bringing your book to a government official to be judged. Ask yourself, however, if some

The Industrial Republic 245

of your prejudice may not be due to your conception of a government official as the representative of a class, and of the interests of a class. In the Industrial Republic there will be no classes, and the officers of the coöperative publishing house will have no one to serve but the people. If they are not satisfactory to the people, the people can get rid of them—something the people cannot do anywhere in the world to-day. You think, perhaps, that you choose your own governors in this country—but you do not. What you do is to go to the polls and choose between two sets of candidates, both of whom have been selected by your economic rulers as being satisfactory to them.

While I do not profess to be certain, I imagine that an author who wanted his book published by the Government would have to pay the expenses of the publication. This would not be any hardship, for wages in the Industrial Republic could not be less than ten dollars for a day of six hours' work. With the rapid improvement in machinery and methods that would follow, they would probably soon be double that—and of course it would rest with the people who were doing the work to see that it was done in an attractive place, with plenty of fresh air and due safeguards against accidents. Under these conditions a man of refinement could go to a factory to work for pleasure and exercise, instead of pulling at ropes in a gymnasium, as he commonly does nowadays. And when a young author had earned the cost of making his book, he would have done all that he had to do. He would not have to enter into a race in vulgar advertising with exploiting private concerns; nor would the public form its ideas of his work from criticisms in reviews which were run to secure advertisements, and which gave their space to the books that were advertised the most. Neither would his critics be employed by a class, to maintain the interests of a class, and to keep down the aspirations of some other class. Also, the book-reading public would no longer consist—as our present society so largely consists—of idle and unfeeling rich, and ignorant, debased and hunger-driven poor.

And then, as I said, there is a second method—the method of the churches and clubs. Out in Chicago there was, four years ago, a man who thought there ought to be more Socialist books published than there were. He had no money; but he drew up a programme for a coöperative publishing house, to furnish Socialist literature at cost to those who wanted it. He got some ten thousand dollars in ten-dollar shares, and since then he has been turning

The Industrial Republic 247

out half a million pieces of Socialist literature every year. That seems to me a perfect illustration of what would happen in the new society, the second way in which books would be published. Such concerns —free associations, as they are termed in the Socialist vocabulary—would spring up literally by the thousands. They would cover every field that the liberated soul of man might be interested in, they would care for every type of thinker and artist, no matter how eccentric; they would offer encouragement to every man who showed the slightest sign of power in any field. The only reason we do not have many times as many of these associations as we have now, is simply that those people who really care about the higher things of life are almost invariably poor and helpless.

One of the curious things which I have observed about those who pick flaws in the suggestions of the Socialist, is how seldom it ever occurs to them to apply their own tests to the present system of things. How is it with art and literature production now—are all the conditions quite free from objection? Is the man of genius always encouraged and protected, and set free to develop his powers?

In the *North American Review* a couple of years ago there appeared an article by Mrs. Gertrude Atherton, in which she set forth her opinion that "American literature to-day is the most timid, the most anæmic, the most lacking in individualities, the most bourgeois, that any country has ever known." This seemed to perplex Mrs. Atherton very much—she could not comprehend why such a very great country should have a "bourgeois" literature. I replied to her in a paper which was published in *Collier's Weekly*, in which I maintained that "American literature is the most bourgeois that any country has ever known, simply because American life is the most bourgeois that any country has ever known." I shall quote a few paragraphs from the essay, which began with an attempt to define the word "bourgeois":

It signifies, in a sentence, that type of civilisation, of law and convention, which was made necessary by the economic struggle, and which is now maintained by the economic victors for their own comfort and the perpetuation of their power. The *bourgeoisie*, or middle class, is that class which, all over the world, takes the sceptre of power as it falls from the hands of the political aristocracy; which has the skill and cunning to survive in the free-for-all combat which follows upon the political revolution. Its dominion is based upon wealth; and hence the determining characteristic of the bourgeois society is its regard for wealth. To it, wealth is power, it is the end and goal of things. The aristocrat knew nothing of the possibility of revolution, and so he was bold and gay. The bourgeois *does* know about the possibility of revolution, and so it is that Mrs. Atherton finds that our literature is "timid." She finds it "anæmic," simply because the bourgeois ideal knows nothing of the spirit, and tolerates intellectual activity only for the ends of commerce and material welfare. She finds also that it "bows before the fetich of the body," and she is much perplexed by the discovery. She does not seem to understand that the bourgeois represents an achievement of the body, and that all that he knows in the world is body. He is well fed himself, his wife is stout, and his children are fine and vigorous. He lives in a big house, and wears the latest thing in clothes; his civilisation furnishes these to every one—at least to every one who amounts to anything; and beyond that he understands nothing—save only the desire to be entertained. It is for entertainment that he buys books, and as entertainment that he regards them; and hence another characteristic of the bourgeois literature is its lack of seriousness. The bourgeois writer has a certain kind of seriousness, of course—the seriousness of a hungry man seeking his dinner; but the seriousness of the artist he does not know. He will roar you as gently as any sucking dove, he will also wring tears from your eyes or thrill you with terror, according as the fashion of the hour suggests; but he knows exactly why he does these things, and he can do them between chats at his club. If you expected him to act like his heroes, he would think that you were mad.

The basis of a bourgeois society is cash payment; it recognises only the accomplished fact. To be a Milton with a "Paradise Lost" in your pocket is to be a tramp: to be a great author in the bourgeois literary world is to have sold a hundred thousand copies, and to have sold them within memory—that is, a year or two. With the bourgeois, success is success, and there is no going behind the returns; to discriminate between different kinds of success would be to introduce new and dangerous distinctions. As Mr. John L. Sullivan once phrased it: "A big man is a big man, it don't matter if he's a prize-fighter or a president." Mr. John L. Sullivan is a big man himself; so is Mr. Frank Munsey, and so was Mr. Henry Romeike, and so was Senator Hanna. So are they all, all honourable men, and when you look up in "Who's Who," you find that they are there.

The bourgeois ideal is a perfectly definite and concrete one: it has mostly all been attained—there are only a few small details left to be attended to, such as the cleaning of the streets and the suppressing of the labour unions. Thus there is no call for perplexity, and no use for anything hard to understand. Originality is superfluous, and eccentricity is anathema. The world is as it always has been, and human nature will always be as it is; the thing to do is to find out what the public likes. The public likes pathos and the homely virtues; and so we give it "Eben Holden" and "David Harum." The public likes high life, and so we give it Richard Harding Davis and Marie Corelli. The public does *not* like passion; it likes sentiment, however—it even likes heroics, provided they are conventionalised, and so to amuse it we turn all history into a sugar-coated romance. The public's strong point is love, and we lay much stress upon the love-element—though with limitations, needless to say. The idea of love as a serious problem among men and women is dismissed, because the social organisation enables us to satisfy our passions with the daughters of the poor. Our own daughters know nothing about passion, and we ourselves know it only as an item in our bank accounts. To the bourgeois young lady—the Gibson girl, as she is otherwise known—literary love is a sentiment, ranking with a box of bonbons, and actual love is a class marriage with an artifically restricted progeny.

These which have been described are the positive and more genial aspects of the bourgeois civilisation; the savage and terrible remain to be mentioned. For it must be understood that this civilisation of comfort and respectability furnishes its good things only to a class, and to an exceedingly small class. The majority of mankind it pens up in filthy hovels and tenements, to feed upon husks and rot in misery. This was once easy, but now it is growing harder —and thus little by little the *bourgeoisie* is losing its temper. Just now it is like a fat poodle by a stove—you think it is asleep and venture to touch it, when quick as a flash it has put its fangs in you to the bone.

The bourgeois civilisation is, in one word, an organised system of repression. In the physical world it has the police and the militia, the bludgeon, the bullet, and the jail; in the world of ideas it has the political platform, the school, the college, the press, the church—and literature. The bourgeois controls these things precisely as he controls the labour of society, by his control of the purse-strings. Unless proper candidates are named by political parties, there are no campaign funds; unless proper teachers and college presidents are chosen, there are no endowments. Thus it happens

The Industrial Republic

that our students are taught a political economy carefully divorced, not merely from humanity, but also from science, history, and sense; any other kind of political economy the student sometimes despises—more commonly he does not even know that it exists. And it is just the same with the churches and with theology. We have at present established in this land a religion which exists in the name of the world's greatest revolutionist, the founder of the Socialist movement; this man denounced the bourgeois and the bourgeois ideal more vehemently than ever it has since been denounced—declaring in plain words that no bourgeois could get into Heaven; and yet his church is to-day, in all its forms, and in every civilised land, the main pillar of bourgeois society!

With the press the bourgeois has a still more direct method than endowment; the press he owns. All the daily newspapers in New York, for instance, are the property of millionaires, and are run by them in their own interests, exactly the same as their stables or their *cuisine*. That does not mean, of course, that many of their journalistic menials are not sincere—it does not mean that the college presidents and clergymen may not be sincere. One of the quaintest things about the bourgeois editor, the bourgeois college president, the bourgeois clergyman, is the whole-souled naïveté with which he takes it for granted that just as all civilisation exists for the comfort of the bourgeois, so also all truth must necessarily be such as the bourgeois would desire it to be.

And then there is literature. The bourgeois recognises the novelist and the poet as a means of amusement somewhat above the prostitute, and about on a level with the music-hall artist; he recognises the essayist, the historian, and the publicist as agents of bourgeois repression equally as necessary as the clergyman and the editor. To all of them he grants the good things of the bourgeois life, a bourgeois home with servants who know their places, and a bourgeois club with smiling and obsequious waiters. They may even, on state occasions, become acquainted with the bourgeois magnates, and touch the gracious fingers of the magnates' pudgy wives. There is only one condition, so obvious that it hardly needs to be mentioned—they must be bourgeois, they must see life from the bourgeois point of view. Beyond that there is not the least restriction; the novelist, for instance, may roam the whole of space and time—there is nothing in life that he may not treat, provided only that he be bourgeois in his treatment. He may show us the olden time, with noble dames and

bear to starve longer than the world can bear to let him starve, is welcome to try it. Letting things starve is the specialty of the bourgeois society—the vast majority of the creatures in it are starving all the time."

So much for things as they are. The Revolution will, of course, not change our present bourgeois people—except that it will scare them thoroughly, and make them teachable. But it will bring to the front an enormous class of people to whom life is a new and wondrous thing; and their children also will grow up in a different world, and with a different ideal; and so a generation from now there will be a new art public. The people who compose it will not have been forced to consider money the only thing in life, the sole test of excellence and power; they will not have been brought up on the motto, "Do others or they will do you." They will have been brought up in a world in which no man is able to "do" another man, and in which all men stand as equals as regards money. They will have been brought up in a world in which work and a decent life are the right and duty of every man, and are taken for granted with every man; in which influence, reputation, and command are given for other things than money. If it be true that faith, hope, and charity are greater things than wealth, it is perhaps not al-

gallant gentlemen dallying with graceful sentiment. He may entertain us with pictures of the modern world, may dazzle us with visions of high society in all its splendours, may awe us with the wonders of modern civilisation, of steam and electricity, the flying-machine and the automobile. He may thrill us with battle, murder, and Sherlock Holmes. He may bring tears to our eyes at the thought of the old folks at home, or at his pictures of the honesty, humility, and sobriety of the common man; he may even go to the slums and show us the ways of Mrs. Wiggs, her patient frugality and beautiful contentment in that state of life to which it has pleased God to call her. In any of these fields the author, if he is worth his salt, may be "entertaining"—and so the royalties will come in. If there is any one whom this does not suit—who is so perverse that the bourgeois do not please him, or so obstinate that he will not learn to please the bourgeois—we send after him our literary policeman, the bourgeois reviewer, and bludgeon him into silence; or better yet, we simply leave him alone, and he moves into a garret. The bourgeois garrets resemble the bourgeois excursion steamers. They are never so crowded that there is not room for as many more as want to come on board; and any young author who imagines that he can

together Utopian to suppose that these will be the things that the new public will honour and will contrive to promote. The best way in which one can be sure about this is to study the writers who are shaping the ideals of Socialism—such men as Whitman and Thoreau, Ruskin and William Morris, Kropotkin and Carpenter and Gorky. Above all I wish that I could be the cause of the reader's looking into one book, in which one of the master-spirits of our time has made an attempt to picture this beautiful world that is to be. When I met Mr. H. G. Wells last year, I had not read any of his books; so he sent me a copy of his "Modern Utopia," graciously inscribing it: "To the most hopeful of Socialists, from the next most hopeful!" Afterward, I was asked by *Life* to name the book which had given me the most pleasure during the last year, and I named this one. It is, in my opinion, one of the great works of our literature; it is worthy to be placed with the visions of Plato and Sir Thomas More. It has three great virtues which are rarely, if ever, found in combination. In the first place, it is characterised by a nobility and loftiness of spirit which makes its reading a religious exercise. In the second place, it is the work of an engineer, a man with the modern sense of reality and acquainted with the whole field of scientific achievement. In the third place, it is written in a a literary style which makes the reading of each paragraph a delight in itself. It is a book to love and to cherish; one leaves it, refreshed and strengthened, to wait with patience and cheerfulness the hour of the Great Change.

CHAPTER VIII

THE COÖPERATIVE HOME

IN ALL that I have outlined concerning the Industrial Republic, I have tried to indicate my belief that it will be the creation of no man's will, but a product of evolution—the result of many forces which are now at work in our society. These forces we can study and analyse; and in picturing their final product, we are not simply indulging in fantastic speculation, but are making scientific deductions. I believe that we have now in our present world the half-developed embryo of everything which I have pictured in the future; the Revolution, which comes suddenly, and in the midst of strain and agony, is precisely the parallel of a child-birth. In our present "trusts," for instance, we have perfect examples of the centralising and systematising of production and distribution; absolutely the only thing needed to fit them into the world I have pictured is a change of ownership. Again, in the labour unions, we see the building up of the machinery of industrial self-government. And similarly, in our churches and clubs, our benevolent and artistic and scientific associations, we have the germs of all the coöperative activities of the future. In our public educational system, we have a complete and perfect piece of practical Socialism, ready to fit into the structure of our Industrial Republic. In our Post Office we have still another, while in the army and navy we have examples of industrial paternalism which need only the breath of a new ideal to make them indispensable for all time. We saw after the San Francisco earthquake the real use of standing armies; and for such purposes they will continue to exist, long after war shall have become a nightmare memory.

It has occurred to me that in concluding my argument, it might be well to tell of another such seed of the future, in the planting of which I myself have had the pleasure of assisting. I refer to the Helicon Home Colony, at Englewood, New Jersey, where I have been living while writing this book.

Our industries are organised at present under the competitive system; and I do not believe that any coöperative method of production can drive human beings to the same pitch of effort as they are driven by the lash of wage-slavery. So I consider that any form of coöperation in production is doomed to failure, under present conditions; and I should prefer to watch from the outside any attempt to found "colonies" of the Brook Farm and Ruskin type. The case is quite otherwise, however, when it comes to coöperation in *distribution*, in the expenditure of one's income. We are familiar with hundreds of forms of that sort of association—coöperative stores, benevolent fraternities, social clubs and churches. The practicability of any such enterprise depends upon two questions: First, are there a sufficient number of people who want the same thing, and second, can they get it more effectively in combination than otherwise.

The idea of coöperation in domestic industry has been well worked out in theory —notably in Mrs. Gilman's book "The Home." The first attempt to realise it in practice, so far as I know, is the Helicon Home Colony.

The plan was broached in an article which I published in *The Independent*, in June of 1906. In the course of the article, I outlined the situation as follows:

Here am I on my little farm, living as my ancestors lived—like a cave man or a feudal baron. I have my little castle and my retainers and dependants to attend me, and we practise a hundred different trades: the trade of serving meals, and the trade of cleaning dishes, the trade of washing and ironing clothes, of killing and dressing meat, of churning butter, of baking bread, of grinding meal, of raising chickens, of cutting wood, of preserving fruit, of heating a house, of decorating rooms, of training children, and of writing books! And all these crowded into one establishment, in close proximity, and all jarring and clashing with each other! And all carried on in the most primitive and barbarous fashion, upon a small scale, and by unskilled hand labour. It takes a hundred cooks to prepare a hundred meals badly, while twenty cooks could prepare one meal for a hundred families, and do it perfectly. It costs a hundred thousand dollars to build and equip a hundred kitchens; it would cost only five thousand dollars to build one kitchen! But, of course, if you have large-scale cooking at present, you can only have it under capitalist auspices; and so it is associated in your minds with uncleanness, and bad service, and high prices. It takes a hundred churns and a hundred aching backs to make a thousand pounds of butter; it would take only one machine and a man to tend it to make the same thousand pounds, and the cost of making it would be cut ninety-five per cent. But of course you cannot have large-scale butter-making except it is done for profit—and that means adulteration and poisoning! It takes a hundred ignorant nursemaids to take care of the children of a hundred families, and develop every kind of ugliness and badness in them; it would take only twenty or thirty trained nurses and kindergarten teachers to take care of them coöperatively, and bring them up according to the teachings of science.

One could show this same thing in a thousand different forms, if it were necessary; but it has all been reasoned out in Charlotte Perkins Gilman's book, "The Home," and anyone to whom the idea is new may read it there. The purpose of this paper is not to persuade anyone, but to move to action those already persuaded. There must be, in and near New York, thousands of men and women of liberal sympathies, who understand this situation clearly, and are handicapped by its miseries in their own lives—authors, artists and musicians, editors and teachers and professional men, who abhor boarding houses and apartment hotels and yet shrink from managing servants, who have lonely and peevish children like my own, and are no fonder of eating poisons or of wasting their time and strength than I am. There must be a few who, like myself, have realised that it is a question of dragging through life a constantly increasing burden of care, or making an intelligent effort and solving the problem once for all. To such I offer my coöperation. I am not a business man, but circumstances have forced me to take up this problem, and I am not accustomed to failing in what I undertake. I have said that "Socialism is not an experiment in government, but an act of will"; and I say the same of this plan. Having gotten the figures from experts and found out exactly what we can do, the one thing remaining is to go ahead and do it.

I suppose that the average professional man invests ten thousand dollars in a home (or else pays rent equal to interest upon that sum); and that he pays two thousand dollars a year living expenses for his family. Let a hundred such families combine to found a coöperative home, and there would be a million dollars for building and equipment, and two hundred thousand dollars a year for running expenses; I believe that for half the outlay five hundred people could live and enjoy comforts at present possible only to millionaires. I have, however, no intention of asking anyone to risk his money upon such a guess. I write this to find out if there are people disposed to consider the project; and if there are enough, I will have the plan figured upon by architects, contractors, stewards, and other qualified experts, and have prepared a definite business proposition, and a plan of organisation for a stock company.

The Coöperative Home

The following embodies my own conception of what such a "home colony" should be. It would be located within an hour of New York, and would have one hundred families, and three or four hundred acres of land, healthfully located, near some body of water, and as unspoiled by the hand of man as possible. It should have an abundant water supply and a filtering plant; an electric light and power plant, and a large garden and farm, raising its own stock, meat, poultry, fruit and vegetables, and canning the last for winter use. It should be administered by a board of directors, democratically elected. For the management of its various departments salaried experts should be employed; machinery should be installed wherever it could be made to pay, and the best modern methods should be applied in every industry. All its purchases should be in bulk and tested for quality; and, so far as the preparation and serving of food is concerned, the processes should be kept as aseptic as a surgical operation.

We are accustomed to having our buildings for public purposes endowed by persons with a great deal of money and few ideals; and so we consume much space and material and accomplish little, exactly typifying our civilisation. The buildings of this home colony should be of frame at the outset, of simple and expressive design, each structure exactly adapted to its specific purpose. The buildings should be conveniently grouped —those for the children in one place, those for cooking and eating in another, those for reading, for music and social intercourse, for recreation and exercise, in still other places. The greater part of the land would of course be given up to farm and woodland, and to the individual dwellings of the families. The ground available for this latter purpose should be divided into lots, priced according to size and location, and leased to stockholders for long terms. Each would erect his own home, according to his own taste—a home, of course, of a kind hitherto unknown, with no provision for the cooking of food, or the training of children, or other trades and professions. It would be a place where the family met, to rest and play and sleep. It might be large or small, anything that the owner chose to make it—my own would be a four- or five-room cottage, of rustic design, and it would cost from six to eight hundred dollars. Besides these there should be apartment buildings, owned by the colony, and dormitories with rooms for single men and women.

As to the public buildings, there should be a large and beautiful dining hall, and a modern, scientifically constructed kitchen. There should be separate tables for each

The Coöperative Home 267

family, or for congenial groups of people. The service should be unexceptionable, the food simple, but perfect in quality and preparation; there should be a vegetarian service for those who prefer this cheaper mode of life, and the charge for board should be based upon the cost of the service. As to what the cost would be, with a colony raising nearly all its own food upon the premises, I can only submit three experiences of my own: First, it cost me for my family of three to board in New York City, in one room and in the cheapest way, a thousand dollars a year. Second, it cost us, living in a three-room cottage in the country, doing our own work and buying our food from a farmer at wholesale prices, seven hundred dollars a year. Third, it cost us, living upon a sixty-acre farm, which represented a total investment of four thousand dollars, doing no work ourselves but the managing, paying a man and woman five hundred and forty dollars a year, having a horse and carriage, and feeding five persons instead of three, a total of less than six hundred dollars a year. Lest this should be unbelievable, I put it in another form—the total expenses of the farm, including labour, were less than twelve hundred dollars, the income was six hundred dollars, and the net loss, or the cost to us of a year's living, was less than six hundred.

And these figures, it should be explained, included not merely board, but also household supplies and repairs of all sorts, items which would appear in other places in the community's accounts. I will probably be laughed at, but I believe that, granting the land, horses and machinery, buildings, equipment and capital, the members of such a colony as I describe could be provided with perfect service and an abundance of food of the best quality at a total cost of one hundred dollars a year per person.

So much for the coöperative preparation of food. And now for the caring for children. There should be two separate establishments, one for infants, who like to sleep, and one for children, who like to run and shout. Both should be scientifically constructed and ventilated and kept as clean as an up-to-date hospital; the food should be prepared under the general direction of a physician. No building for children should be over two stories high, and the upper windows should be beyond the reach of children; no matches or exposed fire should be permitted, and there should be a night watchman, fire extinguishers, and an automatic sprinkling apparatus. These establishments should be under the supervision of a board of women directors; and the actual work of caring for the children, washing, dressing and feeding them,

The Coöperative Home 269

playing with them and teaching them, should be done by trained nurses and kindergarten teachers who live in the colony as the friends and social equals, of its members. In other words, it is my idea that the caring for children should be recognised as a profession, and that servants should have nothing to do with it; it is my idea that it should be done in a place built for the purpose, with floors for babies to crawl where there is no dirt for them to eat, with playgrounds for children where there are no stoves and no boiling water, no staircases and wells, no cats and dogs, no workbaskets, lamps, pianos, sewing machines, jam closets, inkstands, and authors' writing tables. Instead, there should be sleeping rooms and bedrooms, and sun parlours for nursing mothers; a separate building for the sick; kindergarten rooms and indoor playgrounds for bad weather, and a big all-outdoors romping ground, with sunny places and shady places, swings, rocking horses, sand piles, and all other accessories of a children's heaven. Of course, any mother should come and play with or care for her own children just as much as she pleased, or take them home, as she chose; though I think that no one would care to assist this plan who did not believe that children should be cared for in accordance with the principles of science, and preserved from the corrupting influence of grandmothers and aunts. Of course, any mother who believed that her work in the world was caring for children, and who wished to care for her own and others, according to the methods of the commonwealth, would be free to do so, and to earn her living by doing it.

I have already explained that I should not regard this as an experiment in Socialism; but I do think that those who undertook it would have to be in sympathy with the spirit of Socialism, which is the spirit of brotherhood and democracy. Whenever I have mentioned this plan to friends they have always said: "The great difficulty would be to get together a community of congenial people." It does not seem to me that this would be a difficulty at all. Every member of the community would have his own home, to which he would invite his personal friends as he chose; and the other members of the community he would meet in the same way that he meets acquaintances in business and politics, in theatres, restaurants, and clubs. I myself am the most unsociable of human beings when I am busy, and have no idea of giving up my hermit's tastes. In a colony of a hundred families there ought to be persons of every kind of inclination, and it would not be in the least necessary for anyone to associate with those who were not congenial.

Of course there are people in the world whom we should not want near us at all; but such people, I think, would not care to join our colony. Vulgar and snobbish people get along very well in the world as it is, and do not find it a task to give orders to servants. Those who would be interested in such a plan would be men and women who wished to practise "plain living and high thinking"; and they would naturally wish to get as far as possible from every suggestion of ostentation and conventionality. They would establish the shirt-waist and the short skirt as *en règle*, and would, I trust, allow me in without a dress suit. They would be all hard-working people themselves, and they would not look down upon honest labour. This spirit, if wisely and earnestly cultivated, would solve the "servant problem" for the colony, and solve the health problem for its members as well. I know business and professional men who, when they need exercise, have to go down into the basement and lift weights and pull at rubber straps; and they envy me my farm, where I can hoe the garden, or pitch hay, or pick fruit, and not merely benefit my body, but also put money in my purse. In this community every member would be credited for the time he worked; and it ought to become the custom for the men to help with the harvests, and the women with the preserving of fruit, and the children with the berry picking and the weeding of the gardens. I have no doubt that there are thousands of young men and women in New York City, students of art and music and the professions, who would be glad of a chance to earn their way in a community where class feeling did not make labour degrading. I appreciate the difficulties in the way of such a project; the chances at present are against a coal-heaver's being a socially possible person, and I am not insisting that the day labourers should share in the privileges of the community. But I do think that this should certainly be the case with those whom we select to care for and teach our children, and also, if possible, with those whom we permit to prepare and serve our food; if I am not willing to shake a man's hand or sit next to him in a reading-room, I do not see why I should be willing to eat what he has cooked. I personally know a young man who is studying art, and who earns his living by washing dishes in a downtown restaurant, because it takes only two or three hours a day of his time. In Memorial Hall at Harvard University, in the sanitarium at Battle Creek, and in many other places I might name, those who wait upon the tables are college students; and anyone who knows the difference which there is in the atmosphere of such a

The Coöperative Home 273

dining hall knows what I should wish to attain.

The above article brought me replies from four or five hundred persons; and committees were named, which met all through the summer to work out the details of the plan. In October of the same year the purchase of Helicon Hall was made, and the "Colony" began its career. Six months after the publication of my first article, I contributed to *The Independent* an account of how the experiment was succeeding; I quote from it the following paragraphs:

We made many mistakes; I shall tell about some of them in due course, for the benefit of future pioneers. But there is one thing to be said here at the start: we made no mistake in believing in democratic institutions. It was a point about which the critics of our plan were all agreed, that it could not possibly work, because people could never decide what they wanted. That dreadful bugaboo called "human nature" would wreck us in the end. I, for my part, believed that people in America were used to the methods of majority government, and I believed that if we should apply those same methods in a coöperative home, a group of intelligent and sincere people could manage to solve all their problems. From the beginning our policy was publicity and democracy; and from the beginning it brought us through. At the committee meetings everyone had his say. And little by little you would see a majority opinion taking shape on the question at issue, until, finally, when all had been heard, the matter was put to a vote. There was no case where the minority did not give way with all courtesy. And now that the colony really exists we sit round the fireside and talk out our questions, and as a rule we do not even have to take a vote—an informal discussion is enough to make clear to everyone what is fair and right.

I am a believer in the materialistic conception of history; I am accustomed to interpret the characters of men from this position—to say that competition has made them selfish and deceitful, and that coöperation will make them beautiful and sincere. I think that I can see it working out in this colony. We have founded it upon justice and truth; socially we stand upon terms of equality, and economically we pay for exactly what we get. These are the principles we have built upon, and all take them for granted, and no other idea ever enters their thought.

"But will this last?" you ask. I do not see how it can fail to last, and to grow—admitting, of course, that my analysis of the cause is correct. We did not start out

HELICON HALL

Photograph by Jessie Tarbox Beals, N. Y.

with any enthusiasms and religious ecstasies; we had simply cold common sense; we employed lawyers and business men to put us on a sound basis. Our only real peril was at the beginning, before the colony spirit was well developed in our members, and some of us were tired and overworked; and even then there were no misunderstandings that a little discussion could not clear up. Now things are beginning to run smoothly, and we are realising some of the benefits.

We are as yet in our infancy, of course; there is no one of the departments in which we do not intend to make numerous improvements; but we have got over the roughest parts of the road, and we can begin to look about us a little. We are living in what I think is the most beautiful suburban town near New York. We have nine and a half acres of land, sloping down from the western brow of the Palisades, and commanding a view of thirty miles, and we have only half a mile to walk to come out upon the Hudson, where there is scenery which tourists would travel many miles to look at, if they only knew about it. The hall itself has nearly six thousand square feet of floor space on the ground floor alone, devoted to rooms for social purposes; there is a central court filled with palms and rubber trees, which have grown to the very top of the three-story building. We have a large pipe-organ, a swimming pool and bowling alley, a theatre, and a billiard room. We have thirty-five bedrooms, ranged in galleries about the court, so that we can look out of our windows in the morning and see the sun rise, and then look out of our door and see the tropics. We have the finest heating system in the world—we pump fresh air in from outside, heat it in a three-thousand-foot steam coil, and then distribute it to all the rooms, with the result that we feel as well all the time as other people feel when they take a trip to Arizona or the Adirondacks. In such a place as this we have a comfortable bedroom or study, where we can go and be by ourselves and never be disturbed, for $3 a week. And downstairs we have a huge fireplace, where, if we happen to feel in a sociable humour, we can sit and talk with our friends. And also, we have a dining-room, where a group of cultivated people meet three times a day to partake of wholesome and pleasant-tasting food, prepared by other members of our big family, whose cleanliness and honesty are matters of common knowledge to us. This last-named privilege costs us $5 a week, or $4 if we only eat two meals; and we do not have to add to this price any care or worry, because the price includes the salary of a superintendent and

The Coöperative Home 277

a manager, who work sixteen hours a day each to straighten out all the kinks and keep the machine running.

Finally, this magical building contains a dormitory and a children's dining-room and play-room, where ten happy and healthy children receive their lessons in practical coöperation at a cost of four dollars a week for each child. It was over these "institutionalised infants" of ours that the critics of our plan were most incensed. Several dear ladies who had read my books and conceived a liking for me, sat down and wrote me tearful letters to point out the wickedness of "separating the mother from her children." As a matter of fact, we have five mothers in the colony, and the work of caring for the children is divided among four of them. (The fifth is studying medicine in New York.) By the simple process of combining the care of the ten children we accomplish the following results: First, the labour and trouble of caring for each child is reduced about two-thirds; second, the child has playmates, and is happy all day long; third, we can afford to keep the child in a more hygienic place than the average nursery—we have a pump driving fresh air into his play-room all day; and, fourth, we can dispense with the services of nurse maids, and go away, leaving the child in the care of a friend.

Of course we cannot have everything that we should like in the "children's department." We have to wait for more colonists for that. With only ten children we have to dispense with a resident physician; we cannot even afford a kindergarten. And, of course, we have not the scientifically constructed dormitory of which we dream; we have only a converted theatre, and instead of the uniform cots and the dustproof walls and all the rest, we have to make apologies to visitors. However, our children are all enjoying it meantime; and our five mothers are holding meetings and learning to coöperate.

The other big problem which we promised to tackle is the servant problem. All the world is waiting to hear about this, so we are told; even the aristocracy of Englewood is waiting; the ladies come in and tell us their troubles and ask if we will feed them in cases of emergency. They were even going to invite me to lecture them about it—until one of them recollected that I was a Socialist "of a particularly dangerous type."

We have been only a few months at it; and we have still a great deal left to accomplish. But we think that we have got far enough to claim to have proven our thesis—that by means of coöperation, with the saving which it implies, the introduction of system and of labour-saving machinery, household labour can be lifted to the rank of a profession, and people found to do it who can be admitted to the colony as members. Those who wish to make fun of the idea have assumed this to mean that we insist upon college diplomas from our cooks and chambermaids. It does not mean that at all; as a matter of fact, we prefer to employ people who have always earned their living by doing the work they do for us. It means simply that we look for people who are cleanly and courteous and honest; and that then, when they come into the colony, we treat them, simply and as a matter of course, exactly as we treat everyone else. So far as I know, there is no one here who has experienced the least difficulty or unpleasantness in consequence.

There remains to explain the financial organisation of the colony. The property is owned by the Home Colony Company, a separate corporation, which was formed to raise the necessary capital. The company puts the building in thorough repair and equips it for use as a residence, and the colony rents it upon a three-year lease, assuming responsibility for the interest on the mortgages, the insurance, taxes, and other charges, and paying eight per cent. dividends upon the company stock. The ownership of stock is thus entirely optional.

One may live in the colony without contributing any capital.

The Helicon Home Colony is a membership corporation. It is governed by a board of directors, elected every six months by secret ballot. The only conditions to residence in the colony are "congeniality" and freedom from contagious disease; one may reside in the colony indefinitely without becoming a member, but only members have the right to vote. The conditions of membership are one month's residence, election by a four-fifths vote, and the payment of an initiation fee of $25. The constitution of the colony provides for initiative, referendum and recall of members of the board of directors; also for a complete statement of the financial affairs of the colony, to be rendered every three months.

I have quoted this at length because, as I said before, I believe that it is the seed from which mighty forests are destined to grow. We should never have given the time and strength which we have given to this experiment, but for our certainty that all the world will some day be following in our footsteps. We are living in a coöperative home because we wish to do it—but some day you will be doing it because you *have* to. You get along badly enough with your servants, you admit; still you get along somehow or other. But has it ever occurred to you what your plight would be if, when you went to the "intelligence-office," instead of getting a bad servant, you got no servant at all? When that time comes, you will be grateful to us pioneer "home-colonists."

It is a most interesting thing to watch; it is the Industrial Republic in the making. We care nothing whatever about the intellectual opinions of the people who come to live in the colony; but I have observed that nearly every non-Socialist who has come here has been turned into a Socialist in the course of a month or two. And that is not because we argue with him, or bother him; it is simply because facts are facts. What becomes of the old shop-worn argument that it would be necessary to change human nature—when human nature is suddenly discovered to be so kindly and considerate as it is in this big home of ours? And what becomes of the ponderous platitudes about "Socialism versus Individualism" in a place where so many different kinds of individuals are developing their individualities.

I am often moved to use this experiment of ours as an illustration of what I said in the previous chapter, concerning the difference between material and intellectual production. Here in Helicon Hall we have all the dreadful machinery of paternalism which frightens our capitalist editors and college presidents whenever they contemplate Socialism; we submit ourselves to the blind rule of majorities—we allow a majority to decide what we shall pay for our rooms, and when we shall pay it; to lay out our *menu*, and refuse to give us pie for breakfast; to forbid our giving tips, or whistling in the halls, or dancing after a certain hour at night. And we have all the symbols of oppression—constitution and by-laws and boards of directors and managers. And yet somehow, we are freer than we ever were in the world before; because, by means of these little concessions, we have made possible a *system*—and so flung from our shoulders all at once the burden of care which used to wear the life out of us.

And in consequence of that, for the first time in our experience we find ourselves really free with regard to the real things of life. We have absolutely not a convention in the place. We do as we please, and we wear what we please. We are free to come and go, where we please and whenever we please. We have each our own rooms or apartments, to which we retire, and it never comes into anyone's mind to ask what we are doing there. We may work all night and sleep all day, if we feel like it—so little do we bother with each others' affairs that I have known people to be away for a day or two without being missed.

And on the other hand, if we feel like company, we can have it; there is always a group around our wonderful four-sided fire-place in the evening, and you can always find someone willing to play billiards or go for a walk. And as for our intellectual freedom—you should see the sparks scatter when our half-score assorted varieties of "Fabians" and "impossibilists," "individualists" and "communist-anarchists," all get together after dinner! There are so many typewriters in Helicon Hall that as you wander about the galleries in the morning you can fancy you hear a distant battle with rapid-firing guns; and the products of the industry vary from discussions of Yogi philosophy and modern psychic research to magazine fiction, woman's suffrage debates, and Jungle "muck-raking." And yet all these people share amicably in the ownership of the fireplace and the swimming-pool and the tennis-court; providing thereby a most beautiful illustration of the working out of the formula laid down by Kautsky for the society of the future: "Communism in material production, anarchism in intellectual."

It is working out so beautifully, that the spirit of it has got hold of even our children, and they are holding meetings and deciding things. Of our nine youngsters seven are under six years of age; and last night I attended a meeting of the whole nine, at which a grave question was gravely discussed: "When a child wakes up early in the dormitory, is it proper to wake the other children, or should the child lie still?" After a long debate, Master David (aged five) remarked: "All in favour, please say Aye." Everybody said "Aye."

The above was written in the middle of December, 1906. On March 16, 1907, at four o'clock in the morning, Helicon Hall was burned to the ground, and forty-six adults and fifteen children were turned out homeless upon the snow. The story of our ill-fated experiment is left to stand as it was first printed.